The
Jefferson
Wish

The Jefferson Wish

Book 2

WENDY TACKETT

iUniverse, Inc.
Bloomington

The Jefferson Wish
Book 2

This is a work of fiction. All of the characters, names, incidents, organizations, and dialogue in this novel are either the products of the author's imagination or are used fictitiously.

iUniverse books may be ordered through booksellers or by contacting:

iUniverse
1663 Liberty Drive
Bloomington, IN 47403
www.iuniverse.com
1-800-Authors (1-800-288-4677)

Because of the dynamic nature of the Internet, any web addresses or links contained in this book may have changed since publication and may no longer be valid. The views expressed in this work are solely those of the author and do not necessarily reflect the views of the publisher, and the publisher hereby disclaims any responsibility for them.

ISBN: 978-1-4620-3768-1 (sc)
ISBN: 978-1-4620-3771-1 (hc)
ISBN: 978-1-4620-3769-8 (ebk)

Printed in the United States of America

iUniverse rev. date: 8/03/2011

To Bailey and Morgan,
true dreamers.

Carpe diem!

Preface

While this book is a work of fiction, the information about Thomas Jefferson is as accurate as possible based on our many trips to Virginia, research through books and websites, and discussions with those more knowledgeable about Thomas Jefferson. I hope to engage youth in a historical adventure that will interest them while some subtle learning also occurs!

Acknowledgments

Thank you to my family and friends for encouraging me to continue writing the Wish Series. I also appreciate the support from family, friends, and colleagues who were willing to help in the review process of this book, including Bill Barker, Elizabeth Cordero, Gail Cummins, Connie Doorlag, Karen Markel, and Gail Pond.

I want to extend a special thank you to my husband, Paul, who has been extremely supportive and helpful through both *The Snow Wish* and *The Jefferson Wish*. He was my inspiration for writing *The Jefferson Wish*, as he has cultivated my love of history over the years.

Prologue

You'd think our family would learn about wishes. We ran into a lot of trouble a year and a half ago when my sister made a snow wish that came true. It wasn't just one wish; it ended up being many wishes that came true. Some of them turned out well, like when my sister started going to youth group at church or when she won a new computer or when the best drive-thru restaurant ever opened up. Other wishes didn't go so well, like my sister getting kicked off the dance team, her friend getting suspended from school, and my brother moving away from home early. We all had to work together to help fix some of the things that happened.

Our family always makes wishes. Snow wishes. Blowing away an eyelash and making a wish. Throwing a penny in a wishing well. I guess I should have stuck with a penny. Instead, I used a nickel . . . you know, a Thomas Jefferson nickel. Now everyone must think I'm crazy. How would you like to spend an entire family vacation thinking you've lost your mind?

1

Another Wish

"I can't believe you're going to be gone for a whole week and miss school," whined Allie as she traced a circle on the carpet with her shoe. Allie is my best friend in the whole world. I'm totally going to miss her while we're on our vacation. I wish she could come with us.

I smiled and said, "It isn't that long. We can still text all the time. Remember, there's so much learning that's going to happen on this trip too. It's not all fun and games. I'm still excited, though!"

"You're just so lucky, Polly," said Allie. "Yes, I'm jealous, okay. I wish I could go on vacation. Virginia is so far away from Michigan!"

"I've wanted to go to Monticello for as long as I can remember. Monticello is this mysterious, magical place they go visit every year. Then there's this 'conversation' that they like to go to, which is why we're going now and missing school. It must be really amazing because they keep going back," I explained.

"I just don't see what's so exciting about visiting the home of Thomas Jefferson. I mean, the guy's been dead for like two hundred years. But your aunt and uncle are lots of fun, so I'm sure the trip will still be a blast," replied Allie.

Jason came running into the living room with his duffle bag dragging behind him. "I'm all packed. Are you? I'm ready first!"

I hate it when he beats me at things. We're always competing, and it's pretty even. I'm better at some things, and he's better at other things. I guess it's a twin thing. There was a time, over a year ago, when we stopped competing for a while, but that was a very strange time. Lots of weird things were happening in our family, especially with Tayleigh, our older sister, and our older brother, Bryant, who left for college sooner than students usually do. It was definitely a strange year.

"You may be packed first, but I call shotgun!" I yelled back.

"You can't call shotgun. Aunt Leigh and Uncle TJ will sit in the front seat," argued Jason.

"Well, if one of them wants to take a break and stretch out in the far back, I get shotgun whenever it comes available," I interrupted.

"Whatever," Jason said. Then he turned to Allie. "Bye. Hopefully you can survive without Polly for a week."

"You just wish you had a best friend as awesome as I am," sassed Allie. Allie and Jason got along fairly well. Sometimes the three of us did stuff together, as long as it didn't make Jason look too uncool in front of his other friends. Sometimes his friend Scott, who we called Scooter, joined us, but he kind of bugged me.

"Don't forget to pack your raincoat!" shouted Mom from the kitchen. "May in Virginia can mean sunny and eighty degrees or rainy and fifty degrees. You need to be prepared for anything."

Jason took off running up the stairs back to his room. Obviously he forgot his raincoat. I already had mine packed, but I still needed to get a few other things like my iPod. I started to walk toward the front door with Allie as I said, "I'll miss you tons, but you'll survive. I'll even text you some pictures of whatever we're doing. I have to finish packing. We're leaving in just a few minutes. Have a great week at school."

"A lonely rest of the week is more like it. See you on Sunday," said Allie as she gave me a quick hug. "Oh look, there's your uncle's Jeep coming down the street. I guess you'd better hurry."

I waved at Allie as she got on her bike to ride home and waved at Uncle TJ as he pulled into the driveway. "I'll tell everyone you're here!" I shouted as I ran back inside. "Come on, guys! Uncle TJ and Aunt Leigh are here!"

I walked up the stairs to my room to finish packing, thinking about how lucky I was. I looked into the mirror and caught a glimpse of my long, messy hair. Mom always called it dirty blonde, but it looked light brown to me. I probably should've brushed it, but I had to hurry. I was so glad I didn't have to pack any homework, and I got to miss almost a week of school. Even though I liked school okay, it would be a blast going on the trip, and I knew we'd learn a lot. I'd get to see what was so special about Thomas Jefferson. We were even going to meet Thomas Jefferson. I wondered how the person playing President Jefferson knew how to act. It's not like they had video cameras to record what Jefferson was like. Maybe he wasn't really like Jefferson at all. I hoped I had everything I needed packed. It was hard to know what to pack for when we didn't know everything we were going to be doing. I mean, I knew we were going to Virginia, but I wasn't sure of what we'd be doing when we got there. I packed extra things just in case. Luckily Tayleigh and I wore almost the same size, so I could use some of her things if I didn't have the right stuff. She always packed too much.

"Are you daydreaming again?" asked Mom as she stood in my doorway.

"I guess I was. I was just thinking about the trip," I replied smiling.

"Well quit thinking and get started on that trip," ordered Mom. "Everyone is downstairs waiting for you." She walked over, grabbed the brush off my nightstand, and started brushing my hair. "I'm going to miss your messy hair while you're gone. Call me every night and tell me something special about the day. I'll look forward to those calls."

"As will I," added my Dad, standing behind her.

I hugged them both and lugged my duffle bag downstairs. Jason was already leaning against the Jeep, acting all superior since he got there first. "Wait!" Jason shouted. "Is it a jersey week?"

Uncle TJ laughed, looking first at Aunt Leigh's Chicago Cubs jersey and then at his own University of Michigan football jersey. They both loved sports and sometimes argued about which team was better. Recently, Uncle TJ had been wearing a different jersey every day of the week. "No jerseys on this trip, except on the drive down. We'll try to look like normal adults for you." I didn't mind them wearing jerseys. I thought it was fun. They were really like two big kids anyway. I figured because they didn't have any kids, they didn't have to act like adults all the time. Aunt Leigh almost looked like one of the kids, if it weren't for some wisps of gray hair. Bryant and Tayleigh were both taller than her, and I was getting close. I was pretty sure Bryant was almost as tall as Uncle TJ now. I'd have to make them stand back to back next time Bry visited from college.

Uncle TJ grabbed my bag and threw it into the back of the Jeep. "Two down, one to go," said Uncle TJ.

"Where is Tayleigh?" I asked. Tayleigh, Jason, and I were going on the trip together. Bryant would have gone with us, but he had his final exams that week. He and Tay had gone to Virginia before with Aunt Leigh and Uncle TJ, but that was a long time ago. I was glad Tay was going with us, even though she'd been before, because I really liked hanging out with her. We'd been spending more time together at our church's youth group. Last year, Mom made Tay go back to youth group even though she didn't want to. She was elected to a leadership role at her first meeting, and I think she'd even have admitted that she was having fun with it. At least I got to see her more often. I could only stand so much of Jason because we were together all the time at home and at school.

"She's out on the back deck saying good-bye to Leo," said Jason, making gagging sounds. Leo was Tayleigh's boyfriend. He wasn't too bad. I wasn't really into the "boy thing" yet. There were boys I had crushes on, but they just all happened to be movie stars. Tay and Leo had been dating forever, like almost two years, I think.

"All aboard!" called Aunt Leigh. "The Virginia Express is ready to hit the road."

"Oh wait, I gotta grab my bracelet. I wanted to wear it," I said before running back to my room. Aunt Leigh and Uncle TJ had gotten me the coolest bracelet with a blue stone in it when they went to Italy. I only wore it on special occasions, and I thought this trip counted as something special.

"Move it or we'll leave you!" yelled Uncle TJ. Of course he was just kidding, but I still booked it.

Tayleigh, Leo, and Marli walked out the front door. Marli, Tayleigh's best friend, was still begging to go with us.

"We'd love to take you, Marli, but there just isn't room in the car," said Aunt Leigh.

"I already gotta survive this trip with Polly and Tay. I don't think I could stand it with three girls the whole time!" yelled Jason. "I may be small, but I don't think there's room for anyone else in the Jeep."

"Well, send me lots of pictures, text me all the time, and have a great time," implored Marli as she hugged Tayleigh. "One of these days, I'll go to Virginia with you. Maybe Leo can drive us down there."

"Enough of that craziness," laughed Mom. "Now scoot. All of you, get out of here."

Finally. I hoped the trip would be worth it. I planned to take many pictures, text Allie, eat, and sleep. I'd probably even text Allie in my sleep and not even know it!

—*∕∕∕*—

"I want to listen to my podcasts . . . please! Come on, I want to hear what they're saying about the new movies coming out," Tayleigh begged.

"We'll listen to your podcast first," agreed Uncle TJ. "Then Polly gets to decide if she has a podcast or music mix she wants to listen to next, and then Jason. Is that okay with everyone?"

"I don't care. I have earbuds, so I can do my own thing," I explained.

Aunt Leigh reminded us, "Don't forget that we even downloaded the Monticello podcasts so we can listen to stories about the little mountain and Thomas Jefferson on the way down there."

"Can the learning wait a little bit longer?" asked Tayleigh. "I want to hear the latest Hollywood gossip." I had to agree with Tay because I did love the gossip. While I tended to read, and Tay watched movies, I liked to know what was going on. I didn't think she cared too much about the podcast right then though, because all she was doing was texting. I guess I shouldn't make fun of her for doing that because I was texting Allie. It's not like we even had anything important to say. She was telling me how much she already missed me. I asked Allie to do some research for me behind the scenes while we were in Virginia. I wanted to impress Uncle TJ, so I asked Allie text me some facts about Thomas Jefferson that I could share with everyone. It would almost be like having her along for the trip.

"You did get all the special arrangements made for our visit, right?" asked Uncle TJ, talking a little more quietly to Aunt Leigh. I kept straining to hear what they were talking about. It sounded kind of secretive, so of course I wanted to know. I could barely hear them over the podcast, but I had good hearing.

"Of course, it's all taken care of. They're going to have an unforgettable time," whispered Aunt Leigh.

"What special arrangements?" Jason and I asked at the same time.

"I bet I know," said Tayleigh. I didn't think she was paying attention. She was good at texting and still listening to what was going on.

"Don't worry about it. You'll find out soon enough," laughed Aunt Leigh. "Now listen to your podcast."

———

Close to Charleston, West Virginia, where we were going to stop for the night after about seven hours of driving, a question popped into my head. I'd always known that Uncle TJ and Aunt Leigh—but especially Uncle TJ—loved Thomas Jefferson, but I wasn't exactly sure why. I mean, I knew many of the great things he did and that he was a president, but why him? Why not George Washington? Why not Benjamin Franklin? This was probably going to result in a long answer, but I just had to know. "Hey, Uncle TJ," I called out. He was dozing a little bit while Aunt Leigh drove. "I know that you've loved Thomas Jefferson your whole life, but why? What made you decide to make him your number-one president?"

Uncle TJ chuckled. "You mean you haven't heard this story a million times?" I shook my head. I looked over to Tay and back at Jason, but both of them were asleep. They were going to miss out on this story. "When I was a small boy, maybe four or five years old, we had a collection of history books. I would look at the pictures and read what I could. Sometimes I'd even get out a flashlight and read under my covers in the bed after I was supposed to be asleep. History just fascinated me. Anyway, I remember reading about George Washington and Thomas Jefferson, and I thought that Washington got quite a bit of credit for being so great. I mean, he was a great man, but he was doing what he was supposed to do as a general. Jefferson, on the other hand, was a thinker. He had big thoughts and worked to make some of them come true. He dreamed ideas, then invented the reality. He was the type of man I hoped to be someday."

"You thought all of this when you were that young?" I asked incredulously.

"He wasn't a complete oddball, hon," joked Aunt Leigh. "He did normal boy things like play sports and wrestle with his siblings too. You know, sometimes something just resonates with you and becomes your life's passion. It can happen when you're young or when you're old. You just have to be ready for it."

"I was. I read everything I could read about Thomas Jefferson, the good and the bad. There have been some very controversial things about Jefferson, including his ownership of slaves and the children he might have fathered with one of his slaves. While Jefferson wanted to set slaves free, as he wrote in the original draft of the Declaration of Independence, he also relied on his slaves to operate his planation, so he couldn't afford to free them when slave labor was so much a part of the economy of his time. Sometimes I have to put things in the perspective of the day to try to understand what was really going on. There's a quote from Jefferson that basically explains how he was frustrated and knew that slavery was wrong but needed the slaves to continue the way of life at that time. I think he was a brilliant man who contributed much to the way our country is today, and he represents many of the beliefs that I hold dear. He was multi-talented . . . a farmer, a lawyer, an architect, a statesman, a scientist . . . and he taught himself several different languages. Hopefully on this trip, you'll learn more about him and understand why I admire him so much."

"Probably a little heavy for almost midnight, eh?" asked Aunt Leigh. "Your uncle is lucky that he grew up with a love of history. I didn't find my love for history until I found your uncle. It just didn't interest me that much growing up. TJ brought it alive for me, especially through visiting many of the historical places across the country. That's what we want for you."

"I'm going to pay attention. This is going to be a great trip, and I'm ready to learn," I announced. I really was too. Tayleigh and Bryant loved their trip to Virginia all those years ago, so I knew I was going to love this trip.

"That's all we can ask for," replied Uncle TJ. "We're almost to Charleston, so why don't you wake the others up so we can unload the Jeep."

———※———

In the morning, after a filling breakfast, we hit the road for the last four hours of driving. It was a beautiful spring day with the sun shining and visibility for miles around the mountains.

"These mountains are enormous," said Tayleigh with awe. "My ears keep popping as we go up and down some of the roads. I gotta text a picture of these mountains to Marli."

"These aren't even big mountains here in West Virginia and Virginia compared to some out west in places like Colorado. Jefferson's home in Charlottesville is actually built on top of a little mountain, and even though it's one of the highest points in that area, it's still a fairly small mountain," shared Aunt Leigh.

"You know, we have so much to do on this trip. How are we going to find time to do everything?" lamented Tayleigh. "I want to look around the University of Virginia. I love the University of Michigan, so I'm curious to see how it's different there. Who knows, maybe it's where I'll go in a few years. We get to do some things I'm interested in, right?"

"I want to see what a privy looks like," joked Jason.

"Gross! I'm looking forward to visiting Jefferson's other home, Poplar Forest," I reported. I don't think I would have remembered the name of that house except that Allie just texted it to me. I turned to Tayleigh, "Would you keep your junk on your side of the car!" Tayleigh sneered at me.

"Of course we'll visit both homes. What would the trip be without them? We'll see Monticello today and visit Poplar Forest tomorrow. Today we'll also show you around town and walk around U.Va. a little bit. You'll even have some choices about what you want to do. It'll be a busy day, but I think you guys will have fun," said Aunt Leigh.

"Since you guys were talking about college, that reminds me that Polly and I are supposed to come up with something to share with our history class about this trip. Mrs. Truckey didn't say exactly what we have to do, but we have to do something," explained Jason.

"Thankfully we don't have too much homework in our other classes, so we got that done earlier this week. I don't want to do just a boring report for history though," I added. I didn't mind writing reports, but we wrote so often in school. I didn't want to spend my time on vacation writing even more. "It's gotta be good, whatever it is. We're in sixth grade, so none of the type of stuff we would've done in elementary school. Maybe we could put together a little skit about what we learn."

"With two actors . . . boring!" Jason clearly stated.

"You both brought your iPods, right?" asked Tayleigh, and we nodded. "Hello! Video!" She could be annoying with all of her junk lying all around, but she had many good ideas. I hoped I wouldn't catch the teen disease of being super messy.

"I even have my laptop, so you can edit the video on the way home so it's ready to go," suggested Uncle TJ. "I have some crazy sound effects that you can add in too."

"Uh-oh, I feel an argument brewing. You two better figure out now, before we get out of the car, who will be doing what—who's holding the camera, who's narrating, etc. I don't want our visit spoiled by arguments cropping up all over the place," announced Aunt Leigh.

"Us? Argue? Never," I balked as Jason and I cracked up. We did seem to argue often. Aunt Leigh had a good point because we'd both want to be in charge and do it all. "How about I do the camera and Jason narrates at Monticello? Then we'll switch at the next place."

"You're going to let me narrate first? Is there something I don't know?" asked Jason, not quite trusting my generous offer. "You know what? How about if we have Tay narrate at Monticello since she's been here before? She'll be a great introduction to our trip, and then you and I can switch off at the other places we go. You can do the camera first, and I'll be the director."

"You'll automatically get an A if I'm in your video!" Tayleigh shouted as she flipped her long hair like a movie star.

"This is going to be great," said Aunt Leigh. "It'll be like having a video blog of our trip. I usually spend so much time taking pictures, so it'll be magnificent to have this video memory forever. Spectacular idea, guys! You know Uncle TJ will love to help out. He always has different ideas on camera angles and tricky special effects."

"I have to admit I'm excited about it," agreed Uncle TJ. Everyone was excited about the day's activities. We surprisingly weren't tired even though we started out the day at six in the morning. "You know, it's about ten o'clock. We could go to Monticello first and eat at the café there, then walk around the grounds and the house. What do you guys think?"

"Food! Yes!" everyone in the car cheered. "I'm already getting hungry anyway," said Tayleigh as she dramatically rubbed her stomach and put a hand to her head like she was going to faint.

I laughed. "You're always hungry!"

—◦◦◦—

"Does Jefferson own that apple orchard?" I asked as we passed by the Carter Mountain Orchard on the way to Monticello.

"He probably owned it when he was alive. He owned a lot of property back then. Remember, he had many slaves living on the mountain as well, and they farmed much of it. However, Jefferson liked to spend money, and he kept adding on to his house and going into debt. When he died, his relatives had to sell off much of his property and many of the things he owned just to pay off his debts. He was a brilliant man, but he wasn't very good with making a profit," explained Uncle TJ.

"See this little restaurant here—Michie Tavern," said Aunt Leigh as she pointed to a building that looked like a really large house. "That building was moved here long after Jefferson's time, but it's typical of the type of restaurant where Jefferson would have eaten. Maybe we can eat there later, depending on how long our tour takes."

"This is it!" indicated Jason, pointing to the left. "Monticello is just over there."

"Jefferson also owned the mountain to the right. He called it Montalto, which means high mountain. Monticello, if you remember, means little mountain. The organization that owns Monticello bought Montalto a few years ago and is in the process of renovating the structures on the top. Visitors aren't allowed to go up there very often though," said Aunt Leigh.

Tayleigh and I were straining our necks, looking out the windows trying to glimpse Monticello. "I just don't see it," I complained.

"You will," Uncle TJ said with a smile. "It's hidden by all the trees. You won't be able to see it until we get right up to it. First we're going to eat lunch, remember?"

We went into the ticket office to buy tickets for our Monticello tour. Aunt Leigh suggested everyone go over to the café to pick out what they wanted before finding a table while she finished buying the tickets. A few minutes later, Aunt Leigh joined us, and we ate some sandwiches and fruit for our midday meal.

As we walked toward the bus that would take us up to Monticello, I saw a little fountain area near the steps. I loved to throw pennies into fountains and make wishes. Everyone called me a dreamer, but

I always thought dreaming was a good thing. I took a nickel out of my pocket—because President Jefferson was on the nickel—threw it into the fountain, and quietly said, "I wish I knew some interesting things about President Jefferson on this trip so I could share them with everyone." Allie was already helping me with that, but I figured a little wishing could help too.

Tayleigh walked up next to me and whispered, "Be careful what you wish for." We all remembered the craziness the winter before because of Tay's wishes. We had a family tradition of making wishes on the melting snow, and we called them snow wishes. The winter before, Tay's snow wish came true, which caused extreme craziness to happen. It took a long time to fix everything, but everything that happened wasn't bad. Jason and I got to go to a special middle school, which may have been partially due to Tayleigh's wish—we're not sure. The best part of it was that Tayleigh started going to youth group with Jason and me again.

"Wow, that's practically iridescent," said Tayleigh as she pointed to my wrist. "The way the sun is hitting the stone on your bracelet makes it look like it's glowing."

"It's just my sparkling personality!" We joined arms and laughed as we headed for the bus together.

∾ 2 ∾

Monticello

We walked up the stairs to the bus and saw a statue of Thomas Jefferson. "Let's start the video here. Come on, Tay, say something about how this is the entrance to Jefferson's home and that we're starting our Virginian vacation." Jason was being very serious about his director's position. He could be a little bossy sometimes, that's for sure.

I got down on one knee and held the iPod up at an angle so the statue would seem even taller than it was. "Whenever you're ready, Tayleigh, just go ahead."

"Thomas Jefferson, the third president of the United States, spent many years building his famous home in Virginia, always adding to and changing his designs. The Vesper family is here today to start our Virginian vacation at this famous house . . . Monticello," said Tayleigh as she dramatically swept her hand past the statue to point up to where the house was, even though we couldn't see it yet.

A few people in line for the bus started clapping, so Tay took a bow. Jason and I turned to the crowd and bowed too, just because we felt like it.

"You guys are such hams," snickered Uncle TJ. "Very nicely done, Tayleigh. It almost sounded like you planned to do that."

"Thanks. I think I have this whole narrative going in my head from our last trip here. I'm surprised how much I remember—although this statue definitely wasn't here before."

Aunt Leigh agreed, "You're right. The statue was added when they finished this new visitor's center."

Uncle TJ told us to sit on the left side of the bus so we'd have the best view of the grounds as we rode up to the house. When we got to the top, we were ushered into a line of people waiting to go on the tour of the house.

Jason was looking closely at the top of the front porch as we walked up to the door of Monticello. "Did the minute hand break off that clock?"

"No, Jefferson designed it that way. The clock over the front door was designed to simply show the approximate hour so everyone outside the house would have an idea what time it was," explained Uncle TJ. "Just wait until we get inside and you see the other side of the clock—you'll understand how smart Mr. Jefferson was."

We did another quick segment for our video outside Monticello, but Uncle TJ had already warned us that we couldn't film or take pictures inside.

A white-haired woman wearing a blue dress and standing not much taller than Jason welcomed everyone to Monticello. She said her name was Betsy and she'd be our tour guide. She asked where everyone was from and gave us what seemed like a special smile. Betsy did a great job on the tour explaining about Jefferson's entry room and how it served as a museum for his guests, especially highlighting the Lewis and Clark expedition. I remember studying about that at the beginning of the school year, and Jason even did a report on Sacajawea. I noticed a display with a large coin, about five or six inches across, that looked familiar. I waved Uncle TJ over to me.

"Don't you have that coin at home, but smaller?" I whispered. He put his hand in his pocket, pulled out one the size of a silver dollar, and smiled. Of course, he carried that everywhere with him. How could I have forgotten? It said in the display that it was one of the Peace Medals that Jefferson gave to Lewis and Clark for trading with the natives as they ventured west to explore new territories.

Jason was waving his hands frantically to get our attention, pointing to the inside face of the clock above the door. The clock was much more than a clock; it was also a calendar. There were large iron balls affixed to long chains in the corner of the wall. The chains were attached to the clock itself, and as the clock ran, the balls lowered during the week to align with a day written on the wall. Jefferson had the clock built for a large room, and he figured out how to make it work for an entire week at Monticello; he drilled a hole in the floor to finish out the week by putting Saturday in the basement. I wouldn't have wanted to be the one who had to wind that clock each week. I had no idea how they got those heavy balls back up to the top of the wall next to Sunday. Pretty ingenious though.

We continued the tour, and Uncle TJ started beaming as we walked into the library. We all knew it was his favorite room. Tayleigh couldn't believe Jefferson had so many books and that his book collection helped start the Library of Congress. He sold his books to the congress after the capitol was burned down in 1814. There was a long room with books lining all the walls. There was also an archway in the middle of the room that kind of divided the library and made it seem super fancy. Betsy said that Jefferson read books in many different languages and thought it was important that his children and grandchildren learned to read as well. Off the library to the left was a porch with plants on it. I was looking at the flowers and kind of missed what that room was called. Then we walked into Jefferson's office, which was in the corner of the L-shaped series of rooms that included the library, office, and bedroom. To the right, through a doorway, was Jefferson's bedroom. His bed also divided the office and bedroom. It was kind of like his bed was part of the wall. He could get out of bed on one side and be in his bedroom or get out on the other side and be in his office. I guess he was very committed to his work. It looked like such a small bed though. I'd be worried about falling out!

As we headed through the doorway, I heard someone say, "Those boots over by the window in the bedroom are my favorite pair. I put them on every morning after I wash my feet in ice cold water. I believe the cold water helps me live without getting a cold for many years at a time."

I looked around to see who was talking, but I didn't see anyone. I did see a bust of Thomas Jefferson in his office, and I could have sworn it winked at me. I nudged Jason to point it out to him, but he pushed me off and kept walking into the bedroom.

When we walked into the bedroom, the first thing I thought was how smart the design for the alcove beds and closets above the bed were. My room would have been so much bigger if my bed was built into the wall like that. Hmmm . . . maybe I can get Dad to change the layout in my bedroom. Betsy went on to tell us more about the room, including the big skylight at the peak of the room.

Next we walked into the parlor where people would gather for music, entertainment, and socializing. Aunt Leigh pointed out the parquet floor and explained how the man who constructed that floor said it was such hard work that he'd never do another one for twice the price. The doors were also amazing. They were kind of like automatic doors. The way Jefferson designed them—two in a doorway together, instead of one—if you closed one door, the other door closed automatically. Betsy said people didn't know how they worked for a long time, but there was some mechanism underneath the floor that made it all happen.

In the next room, which was used for sitting and eating, Jason thought the dumbwaiter for bringing wine up from the basement and the revolving door for bringing food in from the kitchen were brilliant. Jason tried to take a picture of the dumbwaiter on his phone, but Uncle TJ took his phone away from him. "I just wanted to show it to Scooter," he whispered. I nudged him and reminded him that we couldn't take pictures inside.

Everyone thought the alcove bed and almost circular design of the Madisons' room was amazing because we'd never seen a room like that before. The wallpaper, however, was quite obnoxious. With all the crisscrossing, kind of like wicker furniture, it made me dizzy to look at it.

"When James and Dolley visit, this is the room they stay in. I look forward to their long visits and interesting discussions."

It made sense to me that it was called the Madison room because the Madisons stayed there so often. Who else got to stay in this room? I looked around the room and saw a figure out of the corner of my eye sitting on the alcove bed, but when I turned to look directly at which tour participant was going to get into trouble, no one was there. Must have been a trick of the light.

I couldn't believe how much I already knew about Monticello and Thomas Jefferson. I realized I must have listened to some of the conversations between Uncle TJ and Aunt Leigh. Part of their house was decorated with colonial things, so we grew up learning about Thomas Jefferson. Uncle TJ knew everything there was to know about him. I thought it would be so cool if I knew something he didn't know, and then I could surprise him.

As the tour was ending, Betsy encouraged everyone to take a walk around the grounds and go on several other tours that were available, including the flower garden and Mulberry Row. She reminded everyone to peek into the South Pavilion, walk along the stables, and visit the storage rooms underneath Monticello . . . including the privies. Uncle TJ was looking closely at a shaving kit that was in the Madison room as Betsy was explaining everywhere else people could go. Jason grabbed his arm and begged, "Come on, Uncle TJ, there's a lot more to see. I want to go downstairs and see the privies!"

"Are you sure you don't want to go upstairs?" asked Betsy, now that everyone else had already gone outside.

"I thought you said people couldn't go upstairs because of the fire code or something."

"Hey, Polly, you did pay attention on the tour," joked Aunt Leigh.

"That's true. We're allowed to take small groups upstairs for special occasions. Your aunt and uncle made special arrangements with us for you to be able to go upstairs."

"This was my favorite part of the whole trip when I was eight. It's one of the few things I remember clearly," said Tayleigh.

"Lead the way, Betsy," announced Uncle TJ. "Thank you for taking the time to show us the upstairs. The twins have never been here before, so it's pretty special for them."

Betsy led us up some very narrow stairs past the second level where there were several bedrooms. She explained that Jefferson's family—his children and grandchildren—all used those bedrooms. Because the stairs were so narrow, not every tour group got to go up there, but there were daily tours upstairs. Jefferson didn't want to waste space in the house by building a grand staircase, so he made very small ones. It was a marvel that they even got furniture upstairs because you could barely walk up the stairs let alone carry anything. She then showed us another set of stairs going up. "The house doesn't look tall enough to have another floor," commented Jason.

"Very observant," said Aunt Leigh. "When we go outside, you'll have to pay special attention to the windows. Jefferson deceived people with his windows. He had some very tall windows that spanned two floors, but it can appear to be one long window for one floor from the outside. You'll understand it when we go back outside."

We quietly walked up another small flight of stairs to the third floor. "We saved the best for last. I'm taking you to the Dome Room now," said Betsy as we walked out of a bedroom toward the Dome Room.

We passed a painting of Jefferson on the wall on the way to the Dome Room. It was the same as one we'd seen downstairs. I guessed they had many copies of his portraits.

"My grandchildren, especially Cornelia and Virginia, love to come upstairs to the Dome Room to play beyond the door in the little cuddy."

I looked at Uncle TJ, but he wasn't speaking. Where was that voice coming from? I could almost picture two girls playing with a tea set on the green floor as we walked into the enormous yellow room.

"We're not quite sure what Jefferson used the Dome Room for; it may have been another grandchild's room or a special reflection place. It's just not clear what it was used for, but it is special. I want you to look around through all the windows and tell me if you notice anything," said Betsy.

We were excited to go into the Dome Room. It was very hot in there—no air conditioning like the first floor, but it had a great view of Montalto. I noticed there were windows on all sides of the room, even on the wall as we came in. The windows against the rest of the house had mirrors in them, so it appeared as if you were still looking outside. Just another example of how smart President Jefferson was in creating the details in his house that made all the difference. I imagined having tea parties in there . . . or maybe

Inside the Dome Room on the top floor of Monticello.

dances . . . or lying on the floor and looking at the stars. What a wonderful room.

"I think his grandchildren liked to play up here," I said. "I know I would love to play in this room."

"I agree!" exclaimed Tayleigh. "It's just such a magical place. I wish we could open the doors and look out on the lawn."

Betsy shook her head. "The doors don't actually go outside. Here, you can look. It opens to an attic space." I looked through the door and again imagined Jefferson's granddaughters up there, maybe playing hide-and-seek.

"Can we make a short video? We're doing a video blog for school, and it would be great to show our class this room," explained Jason.

"I think that would be okay as long as you keep your voices down."

Wow! How great is this? "I know we were having Tayleigh narrate, but can I talk in here? I just feel like I know what Mr. Jefferson's grandkids liked about this room." I just wished I had a big, ruffled dress like I'd seen kids from those days wearing. I wasn't the type to wear dresses—I typically went with Tay's same style of jeans and sweatshirts—but a frilly dress would have been perfect for that part of the video. Maybe we should have planned better so we could have had costumes.

"Yeah, okay, give me the iPod," commanded Jason.

I sat down on the floor over by the doors to the hidden attic space and started reporting, "We're in the room at the very top of Monticello. It's the room inside the dome that you can see on the back of every nickel. While historians aren't sure what this room was used for, I imagine President Jefferson's grandchildren, Cornelia and Virginia, used to come up here and play." I laid down on the floor, looking straight up into the dome, and continued as I pointed up, "Just take a minute and dream with me."

Jason picked up on it and slowly panned the camera up to the top of the dome before he stopped taping. "That was great, Polly! A room for dreaming—it's like this room was made for you."

"I know, right?"

"I didn't realize your name was Polly," said Betsy. "Did you know that was the nickname of Mr. Jefferson's daughter, Maria?"

I smiled and nodded.

"I see you've already read about Mr. Jefferson's granddaughters as well," she continued.

I didn't want to be rude and ignore our tour guide, but I certainly wasn't going to tell her that I'd just heard some voice tell me about the girls. I pretended to be too interested in the ceiling to hear what she had said.

After finishing our tour of the top two floors, Betsy took us down all the way to the basement to exit through the all-weather passageway.

"How come you guys get such special treatment here?" asked Jason.

"We've been visiting Monticello every year for many years, but the most special visit was on our honeymoon. I called to see if we could tour the upstairs of Monticello because it was such a special visit, and the director said he'd never had a request like that before for someone's honeymoon. They gave us the royal treatment and made us fans for life," explained Aunt Leigh. "Now they do offer tours to go upstairs, but the timing today didn't fit into our schedule. Luckily we were able to go up there anyway."

"After visiting so many times, we've become friends with some of the staff at Monticello. We don't ask to go see the Dome Room every visit, but we have taken some friends and family up here on special trips. Now you guys have gone up there. Amazing, wasn't it?" said Uncle TJ.

I squealed, "I can't believe we got to go up there! I feel like a princess. The Patriot Princess, that's me!" Of course, I immediately started texting Allie all about it and then realized I probably shouldn't tell her everything. I did tell her what an awesome time I was having. I also had to tell her the new nickname I gave myself, although I didn't think anyone else would call me that. I thought maybe I'd change my name to the Patriot Princess on Facebook just to confuse people.

———

After our trip upstairs, we kept looking around the grounds of Monticello. We found the beer cellar, kitchen, smokehouse, stables, and some servant quarters underneath Monticello.

"While my people—I do not care to refer to them as slaves—are a necessary part of every meal, I am not in favor of too much activity in a

room interfering with the conversations I'm having with my guests. The revolving door for food allows for only one servant to be in the dining room while food is brought in, and the wine dumbwaiter by the fireplace carries up wine directly from the wine cellar."

"That totally makes sense," I said. "The wine dumbwaiter wasn't just about too many people in the room; Jefferson also wanted some privacy with his guests."

"Yes, this was a very busy house, but Jefferson tried to make it feel as private as he could," agreed Aunt Leigh.

Jason saw the privy he was so eager to check out, but thankfully it didn't stink like I thought it would! I took a picture of Uncle TJ and Jason standing in the privy—gross! I also filmed Jason telling our class all about the bathrooms of long ago. "Very few people had bathrooms as part of their house in the days of Thomas Jefferson. While this bathroom, or privy, is underneath the house, it's still protected from the elements and is almost like having indoor plumbing."

We went on tours of the gardens and Mulberry Row, where some of Jefferson's people lived and worked. We were able to video anything we wanted outside, so we filmed some of what the tour guides said about Jefferson's favorite flowers, how slaves and artisans lived, and his passion for gardening. I wanted to taste some of the things growing in the garden, but I didn't think the Monticello staff would appreciate that too much.

The West Front of Monticello.

After the garden tour, Aunt Leigh wanted to walk back over by the lilacs to take some pictures with the flowers and house together. They were her favorite flower. We asked someone walking by to take some pictures of all of us. Jason and I were shoving each other a bit during the pictures, trying to create a little more space between us. After the last picture was taken, Jason shoved me a bit harder and I fell down.

"Not going to happen. Not here," reprimanded Uncle TJ. "All of Monticello is like a museum, and you need to be respectful of that. Sure, we can have fun here, but you can't rough house like we do at home."

"I think the two of you can go sit on that bench for a few minutes to calm down. We're going to walk down to the cemetery where Jefferson is buried next, and you need to show some respect when we're there," said Aunt Leigh. Tayleigh, Uncle TJ, and Aunt Leigh walked around the flower path, taking some more pictures.

"Sorry," muttered Jason. "I didn't mean to get us in trouble."

"How about apologizing for pushing me down?" I sassed back. He didn't even care that I fell down.

"That's what I said! I said I was sorry and that I didn't mean for us to get in trouble. At least no one is crying yet."

I snickered at that one and gave Jason a little smile. When we played certain games, like Phase 10, someone usually ended up crying because they were losing or didn't like the rules or something.

Aunt Leigh waved for us to follow them, so we jumped up and walked over. "Sorry," we said together.

"I know. It's over, let's move on," Uncle TJ said and then started to explain about the

Thomas Jefferson's tombstone in the cemetery at Monticello.

21

cemetery. "It's ironic that there's such a big tombstone for Jefferson. He was the type of man who liked his privacy. Yes, he wrote the Declaration of Independence, he was a great statesman, and he invented many things, but he was a man who enjoyed simply being alone at times, often thinking about the blessings of his family and his country. He designed his own tombstone, smaller than this one, but visitors were destroying parts of it years ago. The descendants of Jefferson had this tombstone rebuilt in its place."

"I thought Jefferson was born on April 13. Isn't that when you celebrate it, Uncle TJ? Why does it say April 2 on his tombstone?" asked Jason.

"He was born on April 2 in 1743, but a few years later, the English calendar system changed from the Julian to the Gregorian calendar. Other countries had made the change several hundred years earlier, but England and its colonies took a little longer. In 1752, eleven days were added days to the calendar to come in line with the rest of the European nations. So, his birthday then became April 13. I like to say that I'm born on the average of his two birthdays—April 7," explained Uncle TJ. Aunt Leigh smiled. I was sure she's heard that story a million times.

"Dabney and I promised that we'd be buried together underneath the big oak tree here. I buried him myself, as he died at a young age."

"Who said that?" I asked, looking around. I squinted into the sun, looking near Jefferson's tombstone, blinking my eyes to try to clear them of what I was seeing. There was a man standing there in a long coat and short pants. His head was bowed, and he was holding an odd hat in his hands.

"Who said what?" asked Jason. "Uncle TJ was telling us about the tombstone. Are you spacing out again?"

I pointed at the tombstone only to see that the man was now gone, and I couldn't see him anywhere. How did he get out of the cemetery so quickly? "I guess so. I swear I heard someone saying that a guy named Dabney is buried here," I stammered.

"You're absolutely right," said Aunt Leigh as she pointed to Dabney's name on a tombstone near Jefferson's.

Uncle TJ continued, "Dabney Carr was Jefferson's best friend when they were growing up. He also married Jefferson's sister. There was a tree here that they used to study under together, and they promised to be buried underneath it when they died. Dabney died when he was a young man, so Jefferson kept his promise and created the family cemetery under that tree." Jason quietly filmed Uncle TJ as he explained the relationship between the two best friends.

"I guess I've listened to you both a lot over the years about Jefferson and I remember some of it," I said as I smiled at my aunt and uncle. I decided not to tell them about what was really going on. It was one thing to hear voices but another thing to see things . . . ghosts.

"Or Allie has been texting you information about Jefferson. I've been watching you text. I know what's going on," laughed Tayleigh.

I snickered uncomfortably. "You caught me." I didn't want to talk about it anymore. Maybe if I ignored it, it would all go away.

"More important than this whole Dabney thing, do we have to walk down the mountain on this path or is the bus going to pick us up?" Jason whined. "I'm tired of walking."

"Well, we're already about a third of the way down the little mountain, and the rest of the walk is a quaint little path through the woods. It's up to you guys," answered Aunt Leigh.

"We're walking. Come on, Jason, you'll like the walk . . . if you can make it that far," Tayleigh challenged as she grabbed his arm. Jason really must have been on vacation. He ran track, so I couldn't imagine he was really tired of walking when we hadn't walked all that much.

I didn't know about Jason, but I loved the walk. There were strange vines growing up around many of the trees—so beautiful. The woods were so thick that you couldn't see the house or the visitor's center. I could almost imagine what it was like for Jefferson to ride his horse around the trail to oversee his property or visit a friend. I couldn't see any signs of civilization at all, and it was so quiet.

"Are you coming or what?" hollered Jason. I didn't even realize I had sat down on one of the wooden benches along the way. I was just looking up at the ceiling of tree branches and leaves and across at the expanse of fallen trees, overgrown myrtle, and scurrying squirrels. So peaceful.

"We can take a minute and enjoy the solitude," declared Aunt Leigh. "Everything doesn't have to be go-go-go all the time." She understood me.

A long walk is an excellent way to clear the mind. I think it is most beneficial not to think at all when I walk. For more vigorous exercise, I prefer horseback riding. That way I can easily oversee what is going on throughout my property."

I watched as a gentleman on a horse rode down the path around us. "That's great that the staff make this place feel so alive. Now I can see why Jefferson would like to walk or ride his horse through here," I thought aloud.

"Is that what this is? Are we walking on a horse trail?" asked Tayleigh.

"Duh, Tayleigh," I sighed as I pointed down the trail where the horse went.

"I don't know if it's exactly where Jefferson rode horses, but it could be. I'm sure he rode all over his property," said Uncle TJ. With that piece of information, Jason started galloping down the rest of the trail.

Didn't they see the horse? I wasn't going to ask. Did I fall earlier and hit my head? What's going on?

—⟡—

When we got to the bottom of the path, there was a Monticello employee sitting there to make sure there were no problems. "Did you guys enjoy your visit today?" asked the docent.

"I loved it!" I exploded, maybe a little too excitedly.

"What was your favorite part?"

"Uncle TJ and Aunt Leigh always ask us that," blurted Tayleigh. Then she looked cautiously at them, not sure what she should answer.

"Everything and everything beyond that!" exclaimed Jason.

"What's that supposed to mean?" I asked, but then I realized he was saying going upstairs was his favorite thing, but he wasn't sure if he could really say that.

"You said beyond, did you? Are you the family from Michigan?"

"Yep, that's us," said Tayleigh. "We had a very special visit."

"I don't think it's quite over. Go ahead and explore the museum a little bit, then there will be someone waiting for you guys over by the ticket office. I'll radio over there and tell him you'll be on your way shortly."

"Thank you very much. Come on, guys, we better hurry. The fun isn't over yet!" shouted Aunt Leigh as she took off toward the museum, smiling at Uncle TJ.

I thought it was going to be a little museum. "This is a lot bigger than I expected," I whispered to Tayleigh.

"There was a campaign to collect enough money to build this fantastic museum. It hasn't been here very long. There are interactive stations, exhibits of real artifacts, a few movies, and architectural models. Go ahead and explore," suggested Aunt Leigh.

"This definitely wasn't here last time," said Tayleigh as she looked around in amazement and started texting Marli and Leo all about it. I agreed that it was amazing, so I got out my phone to text Allie about it.

"Not fair," whined Jason. "I want to text."

"You can have your phone back tonight," said Uncle TJ.

Tayleigh and I started at the beginning of the wall on the right, exploring how the doors to the parlor actually worked. Jason ran over to the touch screen on the left and started making various facts about Jefferson's life appear. While it wasn't a hands-on museum, there were definitely some things for us to touch and do. As I pressed one button, a cartoon face of Thomas Jefferson started talking to me. He sounded like he was just mumbling at first, but after I pressed the button, he told a story.

"The voice doing Thomas Jefferson is our friend Phil Parker, the best Jefferson interpreter around. You'll meet him when we go to Poplar Forest," explained Uncle TJ.

I stood there mesmerized by the little movie. It was interesting how they made it look like he was really talking, but it was also a little creepy. Plus, the voice sounded just like the one I kept hearing.

"Are you sure he's not here today?" I asked.

"I know you're eager to meet him, but we'll see him tomorrow at Poplar Forest," said Uncle TJ.

That wasn't what I meant at all. I'd been hearing his voice, or at least a voice a lot like his, all day. I'd seen him too. I figured he was there and they just didn't realize it.

We walked downstairs in the museum and saw an interactive video wall where we clicked on items to learn more details. I liked the big dollhouse. Okay, so it wasn't really a dollhouse; it was an architecturally accurate model of part of Monticello. I could even see how the house was three stories tall and trace the steps of where we walked. Very cool. Too bad it was too big to fit in my room at home. I took a picture of the model of Monticello and sent it to Allie. She texted back that the model wasn't Jefferson's first version of Monticello, but I already knew that from the display.

Jason grabbed my arm and suggested, "Let's do some filming here. Then we can show our class a bit about the layout of Monticello because we couldn't film inside." He already had the iPod ready to go. I told him to go ahead and do it himself because he didn't need me to stand there when he was doing close-ups. A few minutes later, I was glad I'd moved over to the display about the parquet floor because Jason was told to stop filming by one of the guards in the museum. Oops! Thankfully, Uncle TJ and Aunt Leigh were still in the other room, so they didn't see our mistake.

Jason and I walked toward the center room where we saw Uncle TJ. "We probably should head back over to the ticket counter now," suggested Uncle TJ.

"Can't we do a little shopping first?" asked Tayleigh.

"Quickly. We'll stop in the gift shop for a few minutes now, and you can think about what you might like to buy. We'll be back, so you don't have to buy anything just yet," explained Aunt Leigh. "We can also spend some more time in the museum later if you want."

Tay and I walked over to the store where Jason was already looking at all the colonial games. Tayleigh quickly went to look at T-shirts, and I wandered over to the area set up like a library. In the middle of the library area was a bust of Thomas Jefferson, just like the one that Uncle TJ had in his office. I was looking at the book titles behind the bust as I rested my hand on the top of Jefferson's head.

"From the top of Montalto, I can see all of my Albemarle property."

I jumped and looked around me. There wasn't anyone close to me. I looked more carefully at the bust, thinking maybe it was one that had a button to press to make it talk. I couldn't find a button anywhere. I felt all over the bust, and it was solid.

"Honey, please don't touch that bust. It's very heavy, and I wouldn't want you to get hurt if it fell off the pedestal," said a woman who was working in the gift shop.

"I'm sorry. I was being careful," I explained as I backed away. "I just thought I heard Jefferson's voice say something, so I was looking for the button to make it talk again."

"If you're looking for a talking doll, there's a fifteen-inch doll over in the toy section that says some Jefferson phrases when you press a button."

"Thank you. I'll go look at that." I walked toward Jason. "Jase, the weirdest thing just happened to me—"

"Come on, everyone, we need to get over to the ticket office now," said Aunt Leigh as she rounded us all up.

———— ✂ ————

"Good to see you again, my Michigan friends," said Betsy, our house tour guide. "Just wait until you see our special treat—you're going to enjoy it! Do you see that mountain over yonder?"

"Do you mean Montalto?" asked Jason.

"Wow, you guys have been doing your homework. You're right, that's Montalto, also known as Brown's Mountain. We've bought that mountain and are in the process of renovating the house on top. It will open soon as a conference center. We offer some special tours up there, and we decided to do a special tour for our favorite visitors from Michigan." Betsy then led us to a different Monticello bus that was there just to take us up to Montalto. "Now just sit back and relax. I'll share a little bit about the mountain once we get inside the gates."

"I purchased as much of the mountain as I could see and one hundred yards beyond that."

I turned around, expecting to see that Jefferson impersonator sitting on the back of the bus, but no one was there. I turned back around and looked at Uncle TJ to see if he was playing a trick on me, but he was listening intently to Betsy.

"Do you mind if I film some of what you say about Montalto?" asked Jason. "It's for that school project we were telling you about."

"It's not every day I get to star in a school project," said Betsy.

I was sitting behind Uncle TJ on the bus, so I tapped him on the shoulder. "Did Jefferson really put his feet in cold water every morning?"

"He sure did. That was before he even got out of bed. He had one of his servants bring him a tub of cold water because he thought it would help prevent him from getting sick. I guess it must have worked because he lived to be very old for his time. Did you read that in one of the books we've given to you?"

"No, I just heard it somewhere. Maybe I heard it in the museum." I was completely confused. Who could have said that? I honestly did hear someone say that in the house. At least it couldn't have just been in my mind because Uncle TJ said it's true, and I know I didn't make it up.

"I think it was mentioned on our tour," whispered Aunt Leigh.

"A little bit, but I knew more about it than that," I explained.

". . . but he never got around to building it," continued Betsy. I realized I'd better pay attention. I had no idea what she was talking about. "Instead the land was left without any structure on it, but we're sure Mr. Jefferson used the natural resources the land provided."

"I can see buildings up there," said Jason. "How could someone else have built something on Jefferson's property?"

"When Mr. Jefferson died, his property had to be sold to pay off his debts. He owed a lot of money when he died. Later, a man named Mr. Brown bought the mountain, and the people in Charlottesville started calling it Brown's Mountain. He built a rather large house at the top and a few other buildings. In recent years, graduate students from the University of Virginia have even lived up there."

"Wow, it would be so amazing to live up here and be able to look down to see all of Albemarle County," I wistfully dreamed.

"Good job remembering that name—it doesn't roll off the tongue so easily. You can almost imagine how it was in colonial days, too, from up here," started Aunt Leigh.

"Look to the east," continued Uncle TJ. "You can see how flat it is and how easily settlers could have traveled until this area right here where the mountains start. Imagine them trying to travel over the mountains."

"That's why Charlottesville is such a big city for this area," said Tayleigh. "It must be because people couldn't go any further west."

How does she do that? She's texting like crazy to Marli and Leo, yet she says something smart when I don't even think she's paying attention.

"Tay, hand it over," ordered Aunt Leigh. "We're here on a vacation together, and I'd like for all of us to spend time together. Polly, give me yours too. We'll give everyone their cell phones back in the evening, but let's go without them during the day and enjoy each other's company."

We knew that was going to happen. Uncle TJ and Aunt Leigh took our cell phones away a lot. I guess we all did text quite a bit.

"Let me say good-bye to everyone," whined Tayleigh.

"But Allie is helping on this trip. She's learning a lot about Jefferson, too, and sharing things with me that I didn't know," I explained.

"If you pay attention on the trip, you'll learn things that even Allie can't find out on the Internet, and you'll learn it firsthand. Tayleigh, you have one minute," said Uncle TJ. "I apologize, Betsy. Please continue what you were telling us."

"For a time, that was true—about the settlers, that is—but they also went north and south and eventually went further west," explained Betsy. "Our little town was very fortunate, though, especially with two presidents living right in town and another one only thirty miles away. Look to the east there and you can see President Monroe's house too."

"I can look from here and see my Shadwell as well as my Monticello. It feels like home to me."

"There's that man again!" I shouted, pointing just beyond where Aunt Leigh was standing. He was looking out over the valley below with his back turned to us.

"How can you see a man way down there?" asked Aunt Leigh. "You must have really good vision."

"No, the man that was . . . nothing. Wait, what's Shadwell?" I asked.

"It's just over yonder," Betsy said, pointing. "There's no structure there now, but you can see a clearing in the grassy hill where Shadwell used to be. That's where Thomas Jefferson was born."

"Hey, what's this?" asked Jason as he was picking at something on one of the large stones.

"Jason, leave it alone. It's part of the life on the mountain, not for you to destroy," said Uncle TJ.

"It's a type of moss that grows up here," said Betsy. "You should see it in another few weeks; it's so pretty as it covers most of the rocks. Just be careful as you walk along those rocks because the moss can make them slippery."

"The view is amazing from up here. I can almost imagine that there's an ocean to the east," exclaimed Tayleigh. "This is just so cool!

I'm so glad we're doing some things I didn't do before so it makes this trip special too."

"Isn't it special enough because I'm here?" asked Jason, putting on his innocent face.

"It does kind of look like an ocean, doesn't it?" said Uncle TJ. "But then look to the west and all you see are mountains. What a view indeed!"

"Let's walk to the other side of the house, and you can get a good view of Charlottesville. We'll see who can find the University of Virginia," suggested Betsy.

Betsy didn't know us very well. Jason and I took off running around the house to see who could find U.Va. first. I pointed out a building that was white and round with columns, and Jason pointed out something that looked like a football field. It was all so far away that it was hard to tell without binoculars.

"You're both right. Polly, that's the Rotunda, which is really the center of the grounds, and was designed by Jefferson. There used to be a beautiful library in that building, but now it's primarily used as a meeting space and for special events. You can even go on a tour there. Jason, you found the football field, which is also part of the grounds, just a little further away from the main portion of the university."

"Your aunt and I have been to a football game and a concert at that football field," bragged Uncle TJ. "We saw Western Michigan University play football against U.Va., and we saw U2 in concert there."

"Even though WMU lost, I wore my Western football jersey with pride and yelled so loudly I just about lost my voice. It's a beautiful stadium," said Aunt Leigh. "Okay, now let's take a few group pictures with the city and mountains in the background. Betsy, do you mind taking the pictures?"

"No problem. We have a bench right over here that several of you can sit on if you want. And if you turn just a little bit, you'll have another wonderful site in the background of your picture."

Tayleigh squealed, "It's Monticello! I see Monticello!" Sure enough, there it was. It looked so tiny from up there, but what a view.

"I think this should be the opening to our video—a view of the entire area. Let me set up the shot. It'll only take a few minutes," said Jason.

"No problem, you take your time," offered Betsy.

"You know, being up here makes me think of a song that my grandpa always sang to me," Aunt Leigh reflected. "It's just so beautiful up here, with such an amazing view everywhere you look, and it just makes me happy. When I was little, my grandpa would sing, 'You are my sunshine,' so that's kind of become my happy song."

"No offense, Aunt Leigh, but please don't start singing. I don't need that on our video," laughed Jason. Her singing wasn't the greatest. We took a few more pictures, added some audio to the video, and then Jason jumped up on a large rock for a different angle on the video.

"Slippery, remember?" I yelled to him. Sometimes brothers aren't the smartest things around. Before I even got the words out of my mouth, he slipped on the moss and fell. We all ran over to him to see how he was.

"No filming right now, this director is in pain," Jason winced. He was holding his ankle and rocking back and forth. "I'm fine. Leave me alone." I didn't think he was hurt too badly. I thought he was more embarrassed that he actually fell. He was already trying to stand up on it.

"We need to get that taken care of," instructed Aunt Leigh. "Nothing feels broken, but it wouldn't hurt to get some ice on it."

Betsy waved the bus driver to back the bus up so Jason wouldn't have to walk too far. "We have a first aid kit down at the visitor's center," she offered.

"I think I'd feel better if we got it wrapped up to hold down the swelling and put some ice on it," said Aunt Leigh.

"I'm fine now. It was nothing," said Jason as he hobbled toward the bus. I noticed a tear run down the side of his face. I guess it did hurt more than he was letting on. I decided maybe I'd be civil to him for a little while. Uncle TJ lifted Jason up and carried him the rest of the way.

—⁓—

We sat by the fountain as we waited for Aunt Leigh and Jason to come back. Maybe I should toss in another nickel and wish for Jason to feel better. Betsy had taken them into a back room to get the first aid kit. We got our phones back for a little while so Tayleigh and I could text Marli and Allie as we waited, but Uncle TJ still tried to engage us in some trivia about Monticello. It's not like we were ignoring him, but we missed our besties. After a while, Jason finally limped out with his ankle wrapped up in a bandage. Aunt Leigh had a bag of ice that I was sure she was going to make him use as soon as he sat down.

"Stop looking at me like that," Jason demanded gruffly. I realized he was going to be a bit moody. "I want to go into the gift shop and buy that talking Jefferson."

"Sounds good. I want the pen and stationary set," I added.

Tayleigh said, "I'm thinking about a T-shirt and a book bag and a mug and some earrings and a two-dollar bill and—"

"Hey, slow down, girl!" laughed Aunt Leigh. "You each brought some money to spend on this trip, and we're not going to tell you how to spend it. But remember, we have more places to go, so if you spend all your money here, then you're done. I have to admit, there are a lot of things I wish I could buy here too!"

Uncle TJ was looking at some of the new books that had been released about Thomas Jefferson. He had a bookcase in his office full of Jeffersonian books. I didn't know how he remembered which ones he had and which ones he still needed.

"I thought I had nine to ten thousand books to provide for the new Library of Congress, but there ended up being 6,487 volumes that I sent from Monticello for our government to use."

"How did you make that bust talk, Uncle TJ? I can't find a button on it anywhere," I asked as I was examining the Jefferson bust in the gift store's library area again.

"It doesn't talk, Polly, it's made out of stone. There's no gimmick here. It's a replica of the bust that the sculptor Houdon made of Jefferson when he was still alive."

"But, I swear I just heard it say that Jefferson sold 6,487 books to start the new Library of Congress."

"Where'd you get that number from? That's specific. Did you see that in a book?"

"No," I said, getting a little frustrated, "I just heard someone say it." I looked around in the area we were and didn't see any men who could have said it. It was definitely a man's voice. "Can we find out if it's true?"

"Let's look in some of these books here; I'm sure we can find the answer." So we did. It didn't take us very long, and we found that exact number. "You have a fantastic memory, Polly. You probably learned about this in school and just remembered that number."

"Yeah, maybe," I answered, but I knew that wasn't true. We hadn't studied much early America yet in school. I definitely hadn't read it or known it before. I knew I had heard someone say it a few minutes before.

Aunt Leigh walked over with a few things in her arms. It looked like she knew what she wanted to buy. "Have you two found anything to buy yet?" she asked.

"I've decided I want to buy the small Houdon bust," I declared.

"That's expensive. It'll use up most of your money, Polly, but I think it's a wonderful choice."

"It's weird, but I keep thinking it's talking to me. Sounds goofy, right? Anyway, I just feel like I need to buy it," I explained.

"I think there's a small keychain of the bust for ten dollars or so over there," said Uncle TJ.

"Thanks. I'll go look at that. I could take Mr. Jefferson with me everywhere," I said smiling. "Plus I'd save like fifty dollars." While the small bust would look great on my dresser at home, I liked the idea of clipping the keychain to my purse. I knew my aunt and uncle wanted me to go home with some extra money so I could put it into my savings account. I promised I'd put anything left over into savings, but I really did want to buy a few things on the trip.

"I'll go get Tayleigh before she buys all the clothes. It looks like Jason is already at the counter checking out," said Aunt Leigh. "Jason, just how much candy are you buying?"

"It's hard candy like they had back in Jefferson's time," he said smiling. That boy couldn't stay away from candy. He was also buying the talking Jefferson. Now I'd really be hearing Jefferson's voice!

We all walked outside the gift shop, much more slowly than we'd been walking before so Jason could keep up with us, and Uncle TJ pulled his hand out of his pocket with two small Peace Medals in it. He gave one to me and one to Jason. "Tayleigh already has the one I gave her when we brought her here years ago. You do still have it, right?"

"Of course I do! I keep it in my jewelry box."

"It's something special to me, and I carry it with me always. I don't expect either of you to carry it around with you, but I wanted you each to have one after you visited Monticello," said Uncle TJ.

"Can I spend it anywhere?" asked Jason jokingly. He got bopped upside the head for that comment.

3

Beyond Monticello

"We have some choices to make now," said Uncle TJ. "We missed the meal at Michie Tavern since it's midafternoon, so we need to think about what else we'd like to do. We could go walk around the University of Virginia and tour the Rotunda. We could go over to President Monroe's house, Ashlawn-Highland, and take a tour. We could drive to President Madison's house, Montpelier, and take a tour, stopping at the Barboursville ruins along the way. We could check out some of the unique shopping in the area, including little towns like Crozet and Ivy. We could go hiking on the trail around Monticello in the woods. Thoughts?"

"I think the hike is out of the question," replied Aunt Leigh as she turned around to make sure Jason had his leg propped up in the back with ice on it. "Let's stop at Carter Mountain on our way to wherever we go. They have the best apple cider we've ever had."

"Yum! Hey, but what are the ruins? You mean like ancient Greece?" asked Jason.

"The same idea, yes," replied Aunt Leigh. "Thomas Jefferson designed many buildings, using ideas from Italian and French architecture. One of the buildings he designed was a home for Governor James Barbour, a governor of Virginia. Unfortunately, the home later burned and was never rebuilt. Instead of tearing down the remaining structure, it is still there for people to see. It's in the middle of a vineyard now, but it's still fascinating to see the internal structure of the building without any walls."

"I vote for shopping," piped in Tayleigh. "I'm always up for some good shopping, even if it's looking at antiques. You never know what fun stuff you'll find."

"I want to go to one of the other presidents' houses," I voted. "Isn't the whole idea that we're learning about history firsthand? Besides, I think a presidential house will look a lot better on our video than shopping!"

"I totally want to film the ruins," added Jason. "Can we walk through the burnt building?"

"We used to be able to walk close to it, but now it's roped off. You'll still get a good look inside if you want to go that route," Aunt Leigh answered.

"It sounds like going to Barboursville and Montpelier makes the most sense because that covers both Polly and Jason's votes," said Uncle TJ. "We can still walk around U.Va. later tonight; we just won't be able to tour the Rotunda. Plus, Carter's Mountain, Barboursville, and U.Va. are free excursions."

"It'll be more new places for me to go," said Tayleigh. "I'm in. Can we get some food first? It seems like it was a long time ago that we ate."

"Let's see what there is at Carter's Mountain," advised Aunt Leigh. "We can get some cider or something to go with the sandwiches we have packed in the cooler."

"One of my favorite beverages at meal time is cider, which we store in the beer cellar."

I am not hearing anything. I am not hearing anything. If I kept telling myself that, it would come true, right?

We drove over to Carter's Mountain, which was just around the corner from Monticello. We kept driving and driving. It was up really high. When we got to the top, we saw the shop as well as a viewing deck you could climb up.

"What can you see from up there?" asked Jason as he was already limping up the viewing deck. A sprained ankle wasn't going to keep him from doing anything. If Tayleigh had hurt her ankle, we'd be sitting at the hotel right now while she whined the whole time.

Uncle TJ smiled, knowing that Jason wouldn't wait for anyone. "Go ahead and check it out. Let us know what you see."

"I see Monticello! I see Charlottesville, too! The view isn't as clear as it was on Montalto, but it's still good," shouted Jason.

We all went up there to look and take a few pictures. The smell of the apples was really getting to me though. The apples weren't in season yet, but it still smelled like apples everywhere. "We need to get some of that cider soon," I implored.

"I think they use apples from last year to make cider this year," explained Tayleigh. "I read that somewhere once." We headed into the store to look at the apple treats. We settled on sharing two pieces of apple pie each and a jug of apple cider. There was even a picnic table so we could eat there before we got back into the car. "It's too bad it's the wrong season to take fresh apples back with us. Your friends make the best apple pie ever, and I bet the apples here would taste great in it."

"That is true. We look forward to that apple pie every fall. The pie here is good, so you can tell the apples are good, but the crumb crust on the pie the Gravensteins make is even better," agreed Aunt Leigh.

"Can we get some of the caramel corn to take in the car? I'm still hungry," Jason pleaded. I knew it! He was going to try to take advantage of getting hurt by asking for things all the time.

"All right, go grab a bag, then let's get going," conceded Uncle TJ. "Although, you know that caramel corn won't be as good as that popcorn mix your aunt makes."

Popcorn Delight Recipe: Pop one bag of buttered popcorn. In a large bowl melt one large bar of white chocolate, add one cup of creamy peanut butter, and stir until smooth. Mix together the popcorn, two cups of Peanut Butter Cap'n Crunch cereal, one medium bag of M&M's, and the chocolate/peanut butter mixture. Spread on wax paper until it hardens.

We all hopped back in the car, Uncle TJ set the GPS to take us to Barboursville, and off we went. Tayleigh did have a minor meltdown as we drove right by a big mall on the way out of Charlottesville, but I reminded her that there were malls everywhere but there was only one Montpelier.

I didn't understand how people could live there and not just stare out the window all day. It was so beautiful. The mountains were gorgeous! I didn't think I would be able to concentrate at school at all. I would want to hike and explore the mountains or learn to paint so I could paint them or write a story about kids who lived in the mountains. Then there was all of that history. Monticello was amazing. There was just no other word for it. Well, maybe fantastic or inspiring worked too. Social studies wasn't my favorite subject. I liked to read a lot, but history was kind of boring. It wasn't boring when you were in the middle of it though. Now I understood why Uncle TJ and Aunt Leigh liked Thomas Jefferson so much. I felt like I knew him even though he lived a couple hundred years ago. I wondered if people would feel like they knew me in a couple hundred years. Would people be touring my house and learning about what garbage I threw away?

I could picture Jefferson sitting at the desk near his bed and doing his work, kind of like the office Uncle TJ had. He'd be using that copying machine we had seen at Monticello and storing the journals he had written in his little library.

"I am fastidious about details. I keep a diary of the daily weather. I write down every plant we grow on my mountain. I keep a log of all transactions for food, nails, clothing, and the like. I also keep a copy of every letter I write except the ones I wrote to my dear wife, which were too painful for me to keep after she died."

That made sense. That's why we knew so much about Jefferson. "Wait a minute. What does fastidious mean?" I asked, looking at Uncle TJ in the front seat.

"Fastidious means someone is very particular about something," answered Aunt Leigh. "Where'd you read that word?"

"I didn't read it. You just said it," I said, pointing at Uncle TJ. "You were talking about all the logs and diaries that Thomas Jefferson kept, saying he was fastidious about it. Also that he kept a copy of every letter he wrote, which is why we know so much about him."

Uncle TJ laughed. "That's all true, but I didn't say anything about it. No one was talking because everyone has their mouth full of caramel corn."

"The Monticello guidebook is in the back pocket of my seat. Did you read about Jefferson's fastidiousness there?" suggested Aunt Leigh.

"She wasn't reading anything. She was just staring out the window, probably visiting Polly World again," said Jason. I did tend to daydream a lot. My family always joked that I visited Polly World when I daydreamed. Who knows, someday the things I dream about may make the world a better place.

"Polly World is getting a little creepy, I think," remarked Tayleigh. "You've been hearing a lot of voices today. That's not cool if you forget that you've read something and then you think you hear it. You're kind of freaking me out."

"Never mind," I sighed. I could picture everything Uncle TJ had been talking about. I knew he was talking. Why was everyone gaining up on me to make me think I was going crazy?

"Stop picking on Polly, you two," demanded Uncle TJ. "We're almost to Barboursville."

—∿∿—

"Why does it smell like cat pee?" Tayleigh asked.

"Gross!" exclaimed Jason.

"See, TJ, I'm not the only one who thinks it smells that way. It's the boxwoods. They're those big bushes over there. I think they have a very unpleasant smell too," explained Aunt Leigh.

Uncle TJ shook his head. "Well I like them. Boxwoods are very popular decorative bushes in Virginia. You'll also see them at Poplar Forest tomorrow. We even saw them at Tuckahoe, one of Jefferson's childhood homes."

"Are we going to Tuckahoe?" I asked.

"Probably not on this trip, although it could be an option. It's near Richmond. We've only been there once. Jefferson stayed there for a while as a small child with his extended family. We got to see a small building that was probably his first school," shared Aunt Leigh.

"I moved to Tuckahoe with my parents when they had to care for my cousins after the death of their parents. I was very young when we moved there, so it's really the first home I remember."

There had to be a recording inside my keychain. I grabbed the bust keychain off my purse and started examining it very carefully. I couldn't tell where the voice was coming from though. I dumped everything out of my purse on the ground to see if there was anything else in there that could be talking.

"What are you doing, Polly? You're getting your jeans all dirty," said Aunt Leigh.

"I just heard a voice say that Jefferson moved to Tuckahoe because some cousins died. I'm trying to figure out if this keychain is talking or if there's something else in my purse that could be saying things." I realized it sounded kind of crazy once I said it out loud. I looked up at Aunt Leigh, feeling quite confused.

"Boys, are you guys teasing Polly by making your voice sound different?" asked Aunt Leigh. She was so supportive.

I looked over at Uncle TJ as she asked that, but then I realized that Jason was already over at the ruins peering into a window. There was no way he could have said anything. Uncle TJ was shaking his head too. It was true; I was going crazy.

"Did Uncle TJ give you back your cell, and is Allie texting you these facts? There's no way you know all of this about Jefferson," Tayleigh said sarcastically. "I know you read a lot, but I've never seen you read any Jefferson books."

"I swear that Thomas Jefferson has been talking to me. It sounds like I'm going insane, but this isn't Polly World—this is real," I frantically told everyone. "I thought it was Jason's doll that was talking, and then I thought it was Uncle TJ being silly. Now I just don't know."

Aunt Leigh put her arm around me. "You're not going crazy, honey. We talk so much about Jefferson all the time, I'm sure you're just remembering things we've said at one time or another. It's probably getting confusing because we're all so tired. It was a long day yesterday with driving down here and an early morning today getting started. I think maybe after we visit Montpelier we should just go to the hotel room and relax instead of walking around U.Va."

"I want to go to U.Va.," whined Tayleigh. "I want to look around the grounds and start getting some ideas for college. I also want to take some pictures and e-mail them to Bryant. I can tell him I'm at college just like he is."

"Let's table this discussion right now," suggested Uncle TJ. "So far, Jason is the only one who has gotten a good view of Barboursville. Just look how contorted he is trying to film the innards of the building. Let's check out the ruins and then head over to Montpelier. And Polly, don't worry about it. We're all a little crazy most of the time." He gave my shoulders a squeeze.

The ruins at Barboursville.

"What's taking you guys so long?" implored Jason. "This place is so great! I wish I could walk inside, but it's awesome just looking at what's here. I figured out where the stairs were. Come on, I'll show you." Jason stood up by the ruins waving his hands at us. With that kind of excitement, no one could keep us away. I finished packing up my purse and ran to join my twin.

"Look, see the lines on the walls over there? I think that's where the stairs were," Jason explained. "And over here, I think that was the living room. I can imagine a big screen TV on the wall just over there."

"They didn't have TV back then," laughed Tayleigh.

"It still could be a living room like at Monticello where that fancy floor was."

"Speaking of Monticello, do you notice any other similarities between Barboursville and Monticello?" asked Uncle TJ.

"The two porticos," answered Tayleigh. "I don't know if these are east and west like at Monticello, but they're definitely big porches just like Jefferson had there."

"And the columns. Jefferson had columns on Monticello. I love columns," I added.

"I think you'll see even more similarities with Jefferson's other work tomorrow. I can see some design elements that are reminiscent of Poplar Forest as well," suggested Aunt Leigh.

"Quick, give me the iPod!" I ordered as I hurried to film the man who was inside the ropes, leaning on the side of the building.

"I designed this house for my friend, James Barbour. It was one of only three houses I designed for friends."

"I got you now!" I said as I started filming, but then realized he was once again gone. I turned back to my family and saw them all looking at me with confused expressions. "I . . . um . . . just wanted to . . . um . . . capture the essence of the house. Yep, I was at the perfect angle. I was just imagining that Jefferson and Barbour must have been really good friends if Jefferson designed this whole house for him."

"You're my twin, and I probably wouldn't even put a nail in the wall to help make a house for you," teased Jason. I started chasing him around the yard, easily catching him and sitting on him.

"Be careful of his ankle, please," said Aunt Leigh.

"I'd help you, Polly. Maybe not in building your house, but I could be your interior designer," offered Tayleigh. Thank goodness for sisters.

We walked around the ruins a little more, trying to imagine what the governor's house was like before it burned down. Uncle TJ thought there might have been a dome on top of the house just like Monticello. I wondered if the governor's kids played up there too. Jason was cracking me up trying to figure out where the privies were. He had such an obsession!

—◦◦◦—

"Can't we go swimming now? It's so hot out. I just want to go to the hotel and swim. There is a pool, right? I won't overdo it, but the water will feel so good," begged Jason.

"Me too!" I agreed. "I'm enjoying the history, but it's been a long day already, and a swim in the pool would wake me up."

"I'd rather just take a nap," said Tayleigh. "We got up way too early this morning."

"I know we're doing a lot today, but tomorrow will be a lot slower paced. And after we leave Montpelier, we'll head to the hotel, get checked in, and relax for the evening," explained Aunt Leigh. "Montpelier closes at five, so we won't be staying there very late anyway."

"I thought we were going to head to the University of Virginia after Montpelier," said Uncle TJ. "I think you all will enjoy seeing U.Va.

We can show you some symbols from the secret societies, although we don't really know much about them because they're secret." Uncle TJ was whispering in a very secretive way. I knew he was doing it to be silly, but it definitely made U.Va. sound more interesting. Maybe we'd find something that would lead us on a treasure hunt and track down something of Thomas Jefferson's that nobody knew about. Maybe we'd find the secret entrance to the secret society where they locked away college students who failed their classes. Maybe . . .

"Polly!" shouted Jason and Tayleigh together.

"What?" I said, looking a bit confused.

"Yep, Polly World again," laughed Tayleigh. "We were just saying that maybe after a quick swim we could still go check out some of U.Va. if we're feeling reenergized at that point. Jason asked what you thought, but you weren't paying attention."

"Sorry, I was lost in thoughts about secret societies."

"I knew I'd get at least one of them interested with that comment," smiled Uncle TJ.

"Come on, everyone back into the car. Montpelier is only five minutes away, and we've only got about an hour to spend there. It'll be time well spent, though, as it's a very interesting building. It's not the same style as Jefferson's, but you'll still see some similarities. The interesting part is that it's two houses in one. You'll just have to wait to figure that one out," teased Aunt Leigh.

"James Monroe's house, right?" challenged Jason.

"Close. James Monroe's house was the one a few miles away from Monticello, called Ashlawn-Highland. We could see it from Montalto, remember? Montpelier was James and Dolley Madison's house," responded Uncle TJ.

"I'll remember that. I love Dolley Madison! She makes the best donuts," said Jason.

"You think you're being silly, but you're not far off. Dolley was famous for her entertaining, so the company that makes the snacks named themselves after Dolley."

Only with my aunt and uncle could something as simple as a donut also have educational value. I knew they couldn't know everything about everything, but sometimes it seemed like they did. I hoped that one day I'd stump them.

—◦◦◦—

"We'll look at the gift shop when we're done with the tour, Jason. Besides, you already bought a ton of candy at Monticello. Now, come on, the video is starting in just two minutes," I ordered. There was a big digital readout of when the new video was starting, and Uncle TJ, Aunt Leigh, and Tayleigh had already gone inside to get us seats. I was still reading the timeline about the Madisons next to the theatre, and I even found some pictures and a mention of Thomas Jefferson. So, because I was the last one out there, I got to be the lucky one to go get Jason. Yep, lucky me.

"James is a brilliant man, but I think he is all the better for the love and support of his wife. Dolley even helped me as president, performing some of the First Lady duties since my beloved Martha was no longer with me."

"Come on, Jason, it's started early! I hear Thomas Jefferson talking about the Madisons!" I shouted as I tugged on Jason's arm.

"The clock still says we have one minute and fifteen seconds, so I'll just take my time," said Jason.

Brothers! Well, not all brothers. Bryant would have been in there early. He'd want to learn all he could so he'd be more prepared in college. Jason was another story. He did well in school, but if you gave him some candy, a ball to play some game outside, or a Wii, you'd have lost him for hours. I gave him one of my winning sisterly looks and ran into the theatre so I wouldn't miss any more of the show.

Nothing. The screen was still dark, and the lights were still on. The movie hadn't started yet. I didn't understand. I knew I heard Jefferson's voice. "Aunt Leigh, did I already miss something? I heard Jefferson talking about Dolley helping him in the White House," I whispered as I sat down next to Aunt Leigh.

"No, hon, it hasn't started yet. You're right, though, Dolley did help out Jefferson while he was president. She was the ultimate hostess."

I didn't get a chance to ask more about that because the lights dimmed just as Jason thumped down in the seat next to me. The video was short, but it helped give us some perspective on what happened to Montpelier. Monticello had pretty much been the same since Thomas

Jefferson lived there. That wasn't true about Montpelier. Another family owned it for a while and made it a lot bigger and painted it pink. A huge pink mansion . . . weird. I knew Uncle TJ and Aunt Leigh loved all the brick on the homes in Virginia, but it would have been interesting to see it when it was all pink.

"I kind of wish I could have seen Montpelier as the Dupont house," I murmured, not realizing I was talking out loud.

"We did see it when it had pink stucco on the outside. I don't think the Madisons would have liked it," said Aunt Leigh. "We also saw it when they were in the middle of the renovation they've now completed. It's been fascinating to see it at the various stages along the way."

"That's why you guys love going to Poplar Forest all the time, too, isn't it?" asked Tayleigh.

"Very true," agreed Uncle TJ. "The organization that runs Montpelier got some large donations from people who wanted to see Montpelier fixed to look like it did during James Madison's time. Because of those donations, they were able to do the restoration a lot faster than Poplar Forest has. Poplar Forest will still be worked on for many years, but they've made tremendous progress. We'll show you all of that tomorrow." He waved for us all to follow him through an opening in the trees, and on the other side we got our first close view of Montpelier.

Tayleigh grabbed my iPod to film Jason and me as we walked toward the house. I guessed it wouldn't hurt to have a few shots with both of us in them together. We shouted out, "Welcome to President Madison's Montpelier!" Tonight we'll have to post a bunch of pictures and maybe some video on Facebook so Allie and my folks can see what we're doing, I thought. I suppose Leo and Marli and Bryant and lots of other people will want to see them too. I don't know if I want Scooter to see them, though. He was Jason's best friend, and I thought he had a crush on me. I just didn't have time to be bothered by boys; I was much too busy with dance.

"Polly, come on. The tour starts on the front porch," called Aunt Leigh. I noticed everyone else was already on the front porch. Guess I'll take a picture of that, too.

—◦◦◦—

**Montpelier, the home of President James Madison
and his wife, Dolley.**

The tour was very different from Monticello. First of all, there was very little furniture and only a few pictures hanging on the wall. Secondly, the walls weren't finished. While the outside of the house looked done, they had lots of work to do inside. But, because it wasn't all finished, we got to see some cool things like the inside of a wall where there was a rat's nest with little pieces of junk from the Madisons' time and an ink stain on the floor in Mr. Madison's library that could have been from when he was working on the Constitution or some of his other important thoughts.

"I told Mr. Madison several times that there needs to be a Bill of Rights along with his wonderful Constitution. The people would demand it."

I jumped and then quickly realized no one else was started by the emphasis on the word "demand." I must have been hearing things again. I tried to cover by whispering to Uncle TJ, "I didn't realize that the Bill of Rights was Thomas Jefferson's idea."

He pulled me in close, "Interesting perception, Polly. It wasn't exactly Jefferson's idea, but he did tell Madison that a Bill of Rights was needed."

The weirdest thing about the house was the two kitchens. Dolley Madison had her own kitchen in the basement of her half of the house, and her mother-in-law had one on her side too. They both had different styles of cooking and eating, so they kept it separate. We also got to stand on part of the roof, which Jason had to film because he was feeling pretty tall.

After the tour, we wandered over to where some staff was cooking food using old-style equipment.

"It doesn't smell that good," I whispered to Tayleigh as I crinkled my nose.

"I agree," she nodded. "I'm always hungry, but I'll pass on this."

"They cooked with real animal fat back then, so that's probably what you're smelling," explained Aunt Leigh. "Remember, this is supposed to be fairly authentic, so I doubt they're using canola oil."

"Gross!" I squealed. I ate meat. Not much of it, but I did eat it. But cooking in animal fat . . . that just sounded disgusting. Some things about colonial times were fantastic, but other things made me very happy to be living now.

"I'm not grossed out. I'll try anything. Get out the iPod and film me eating some of this old food," ordered Jason. He walked over to the two women who were cooking and started talking with them to explain why we were filming. Fortunately, they were cool about it and didn't hear any of my complaining about the smell.

"These fine ladies, Ms. Payton and Ms. Emerson, were transported here through a time warp so they could share early cooking secrets with us," started Jason as I was recording. "As you look into the hot pan, you'll see what almost looks like donuts. Hey, I was just telling everyone how much I like Dolley's donuts!" Jason cracked himself up, so I zoomed in on the boiling lard.

"They are very similar to donuts," said Payton. "These would be eaten with a little sugar sprinkled on top as a dessert."

"They're just about done cooking. If you wait a minute and let them cool, you can each try one," offered Emerson.

I shook my head, and Tayleigh backed away. Jason piped up, "I'll be happy to eat Polly and Tayleigh's donuts as well." And, he did. He said they were good, but I just couldn't get past the awful smell.

We thanked the women and started walking to some outdoor structure. "What is that? It reminds me of something from a movie I saw with a guy and a girl singing. I can't remember the name," said Jason.

"*The Sound of Music*," I suggested. "I liked that scene, too."

"Believe it or not, it's where the Madisons stored ice," shared Uncle TJ.

"Not," replied Tayleigh. "The ice cellar at Monticello was underground. Why would the Madisons store their ice in their gazebo?"

"More like a temple, I think," said Aunt Leigh. "And, of course they didn't store their ice out in the open like that. The temple building is built on top of where the ice is stored."

Tayleigh smiled, "I knew it! It is underground. That's a fancy entrance just to get some ice."

"I bet they used to have benches between the columns so people could sit out here and enjoy nature. I'd just love to sit in there for a while," I said dreamily. I imagined being an artist and sitting out there for hours, drawing everything I saw.

"Your Uncle Henry thought the same thing when we brought him here last year. I think he wants to build something like this in their backyard," offered Uncle TJ.

"I hope his temple has as many spiders as this one does," interjected Jason as he pointed next to where I was sitting.

Of course I screamed and jumped up. That just made Jason laugh all the more. And, just my luck, he was filming the whole time. Great, the class was going to get a good laugh out of that. He was right, though; there were spiders all over. I seriously didn't see them. Sometimes I think I need to focus more on the now rather than my dreams, so then I'd notice things like spiders crawling all around me. Ewwww!

"Come on, we'll take a longer walk back to the gift shop by heading over to the garden," said Uncle TJ as he pointed past the house. "It's not really the garden the way it was when the Madisons lived here, but it's still very pretty."

"Can I take the shorter walk back? I don't care about the garden. I'd rather shop," grumbled Tayleigh.

Aunt Leigh ignored her and said, "It kind of reminds me of the type of garden from the one Harry Potter movie where Cedric gets killed. There are different paths you can take with some statues and sitting areas."

I liked the Harry Potter movies, but that scene completely creeped me out. I had a recurring nightmare where I was trapped in a maze and couldn't find my way out. I didn't think I wanted to go into that garden. I decided maybe I'd just wander around the front of the house and meet them back at the gift shop. It was funny that the place reminded us of so many movies. Maybe they'd filmed some movies there.

"Polly, pay attention! You're sitting on the spiders again!" screeched Tayleigh.

I stood up quickly and ran over to the group. "I just can't win. I'm a little scared of the garden now that Aunt Leigh described it. I don't want to get lost," I quietly said.

"No worries," Uncle TJ said. "There's a straight path from the front entrance to the back exit. If Jason wants to run around other paths, he can, but it's not even really a maze. Leigh was just trying to make it sound more exciting. There is a large sundial in the middle of it, though. Go on, Tayleigh, just meet us back in the gift shop, with some of your money still in your pocket."

Tayleigh went right, and we went to the left toward the creepy gardens. Whew. Uncle TJ was right, but so was Aunt Leigh. It did kind of remind me of the movie, but it wasn't scary like my nightmare at all. Although, I have to admit that I just walked the straight path from front to back. Jason scurried all around, but he kept talking to us. He was short enough that he couldn't see over the hedges, but there was nowhere you could get lost in there. And, there were some pretty flowers, but there were also more of those smelly boxwoods.

We only spent a few minutes in the gift shop, which Tayleigh had scoured thoroughly for her few small purchases, before we headed back to the car.

"Who is up for that swim?" asked Uncle TJ.

We all yelled, "Me!"

—◦◦◦—

After we checked into the hotel, we practically ran to the room so we could get changed and head to the pool. The room was sweet; in fact, it was a suite! There was a bedroom on the left side with a bathroom, a living room, and small kitchen in the middle, and a bedroom with a bathroom on the right side. Tayleigh and I took one room, and Jason got the pull-out couch in the living room. It was just perfect! Aunt Leigh said the suite was cheaper than getting two rooms, since they didn't have one room big enough for all five of us to stay in.

We went down to the pool for a quick swim.

"Recreation is as vitally consequential to living as learning. The state of your health is very important."

I really couldn't imagine President Jefferson playing around in a swimming pool. I wondered if they played in the water like that during his time. That little pool of water by Monticello was for fish, not swimming. I was glad it was warmer than it was in Michigan so that we got to enjoy the sun a little bit. Jason even brought the iPod so I could film him jumping off the diving board in every way imaginable. What a goof! Tayleigh only jumped in once to get wet and then found a lounge chair in the sun and lay down to catch a little nap and sun. After a few minutes, Uncle TJ and Jason were busy chasing each other inside the pool, and I just sat on the edge with my feet dangling in the water. Aunt Leigh came over to sit by me.

"What do you think about the trip so far?" she asked me.

"Is it really only the first day in Virginia? I feel like we've already done so much. I'm so tired, but it's also been fun," I told her.

"Wait a minute!" Aunt Leigh gasped, acting shocked. "Didn't we explain that you're not supposed to have any fun on this trip?"

We both laughed. When we were little, Aunt Leigh and Uncle TJ would always tell us we weren't allowed to have any fun. We always had the most fun when we were doing things with them, so it was just a little joke. Sometimes we'd be somewhere and one of them would yell at us to stop having fun, and we'd pretend to cry. People would stare at us. Yep, we have a goofy family.

"Sorry, you're right, the trip has been abysmal," I conceded.

"Haha! Good word," Aunt Leigh said as she drew me into a hug.

I smiled. "I've been waiting to use that one. Honestly, I've heard about Virginia and Thomas Jefferson all of my life, but it all seems so much more real to me now. I really feel like I can see him walking around and talking to me."

"It seems your imagination has been working overtime today," laughed Aunt Leigh. "That's great, though. The more everything is real to you, the more you'll remember it when you're studying it back in school or when you're doing great things in the world as an adult. I think the world would be a much better place today if people remembered some of the wonderful ideas that our founding fathers and mothers had." Aunt Leigh shook her head and looked off toward the mountains.

We both squealed as we got splashed with lots of water. "It looked like you guys were having a serious conversation over here, so we had to end that," yelled Jason as he splashed us again.

"I think we're about ready to head over to the University of Virginia. We can find a restaurant around there where we can have dinner. Go wake up your sister and let's get changed," said Uncle TJ.

I woke up Tay and told her we had to hurry.

"We're going to a college campus where there will be college boys; I am not going to hurry. I have to straighten my hair, reapply my makeup, and pick out just the right outfit," clarified Tayleigh.

"You'll have ten minutes to do all of that, and then we're leaving," stated Uncle TJ. "Or, I could call Leo and tell him you're spending tons of time beautifying yourself for other boys."

"Um, I'll be quick," Tayleigh said as she disappeared into the bathroom. Of course, Uncle TJ was just kidding, but anything to hurry Tay along is a good thing.

I'd been to the University of Michigan to see Bryant, and it was an amazing campus. I loved the law library—it looked like something out of a movie. I also thought it was awesome how students lived right there, and they could walk to class or walk to a movie or walk to a restaurant. Everything was so close. It just wasn't fair. By the time you're in college, everyone can drive, so they don't need to be able to walk to everything. I couldn't drive, and it would have been awesome to live somewhere like that where I could have some independence and walk anywhere I want for whatever I needed. The University of Virginia was like that too, but I guess probably most universities are like that. There were many brick buildings there, just like at U of M, but there were also many buildings there that had columns on them, which made me think of Thomas Jefferson.

"Do you all remember that Jefferson designed the University of Virginia? We showed you where he could see the Rotunda from Monticello," said Uncle TJ as we stood on the steps near the bookstore.

"I bet Jefferson had a spyglass like the pirates had so he could spy on the construction as it was going on," suggested Jason.

"He probably did have a telescope to watch. Whereas it only takes us a few minutes to get from Monticello to U.Va., it would have taken him much longer to ride by horse over the hills and through the woods," explained Aunt Leigh.

"To grandmother's house we go . . ." sang Tayleigh as we all started laughing. "Can we go in the bookstore now? I want to buy a Virginia sweatshirt."

"Let's go walk around the grounds a bit first. We have plenty of time before the bookstore closes, and this way you don't have to carry a bag around," said Aunt Leigh.

We followed Uncle TJ around the grounds for a while, and he pointed out some of his favorite parts like the old church, the serpentine wall, and the Rotunda.

"It's too bad we can't go on a tour of the Rotunda, but they close that early. The Dome Room at the top was actually built as a library. It's phenomenal to see and even better when you see some of the unique design features that can only be Jefferson's," explained Uncle TJ. "Let's go inside on the main floor though. I think we can still walk in there."

"Wait a minute before we go in. Everyone turn around and just look," suggested Aunt Leigh. We had to walk up many steps to go inside the Rotunda, so the view along the lawn was great from up there. "This is Jefferson's University of Virginia. The other things we've walked around weren't all here in his time. This portion from the Rotunda along the lawn, including the dorm rooms and classrooms, were what he designed. The larger buildings along the lawn are the Pavilions where professors lived and held classes, as they still do today. He wanted the students to have easy access to knowledge, from the library to the faculty."

"It's kind of like looking out the door at Monticello on the lawn," yawned Jason, acting like he didn't care. I could tell that he was proud of himself for noticing that similarity.

"I like to make you feel like the outside and the inside merge together. I do that in different ways in each of the places I design, but at the University of Virginia, I believe the open space does just that."

"Somehow I think Jefferson would agree with you." I nodded at Jason. "I think he liked having an open yard wherever he built homes and buildings." I wasn't even going to mention that I heard Jefferson say that because I already knew everyone thought I was crazy. I didn't need to encourage that anymore. Maybe I'd just keep what I heard to myself.

We walked inside the Rotunda, only to find out that most of the building was roped off so we didn't get to see very much. We walked around the outside and down the stairs on the opposite side where there was a statue of Thomas Jefferson.

"That's so not cool!" yelled Tayleigh as she pointed to a giant Z on the sidewalk down near the statue. We walked down to get a closer look. "I can't stand tagging, but you have to admit that even the vandalism at U.Va. looks classy."

"It's not vandalism in the sense that you think," explained Uncle TJ. "Remember I mentioned that there are some secret societies that are part of the university?"

"I remember! I've been waiting for this part. Can I please have my cell phone? I really want to text Scooter about this!" said Jason.

"You'll all get your cell phones back later, and then you can update everyone on your day. Just listen right now," said Aunt Leigh.

I pushed Jason slightly. "Get out the iPod to film. We can use this part in our video. Just wait a minute, Uncle TJ, until Jason is ready."

"Film me for a second," Jason ordered as he handed me the iPod. "You want mystery? You want secrets? You want scandal? This is where it all starts . . . at the Z . . . at the University of Virginia!" He was a good entertainer. He could ham it up with the best of them. "Tell us all you know about the Z, Uncle TJ, and all that you don't know!"

The Rotunda at the University of Virginia, with evidence of secret societies all around.

Uncle TJ had to take a minute to stop laughing before he could talk to us. "The Z Society isn't scandalous at all. It's just the kind of secret society I would hope each of you would be involved with someday. I don't know all of this for sure, because it is a secret and I'm not a member, but I can share what I think I know about it. The Z Society is a secret society—its members are totally anonymous. They believe in doing community service and making donations to help others, and they prefer to do it without recognition. Once students who were in the Z Society graduate, they are given a Z ring to wear, so their anonymity ends at that point. The society has been around since the late 1800s."

"Was Jefferson a member?" asked Jason.

Tayleigh hit him upside the head, and then he shoved her back. "Both of you cut it out," intervened Aunt Leigh.

"Well, it was a dumb question," sassed Tayleigh.

"There are no dumb questions. It's better to ask a question to find out the right answer than to make up your own answers in your head. At least that's what our teacher says," I explained.

"Your teacher is right," concurred Aunt Leigh. "Jason, Jefferson died before the society was started, so he wasn't a member."

Jason kicked at pretend rocks on the cement and said sheepishly, "I guess I should have known that."

"The Z Society isn't the only secret society at U.Va.," continued Uncle TJ. Jason started filming again to capture it all. "There's also the IMP and 7 Societies. The IMP Society started a few years after the Z Society and also has a focus on service, but they do tend to cause a little mischief along the way."

"Is that why they're called imps?" asked Tayleigh.

"Makes sense to me, but I don't know," answered Uncle TJ. "I do know that they've done some things over the years they've gotten in trouble for, and the members aren't quite as anonymous as the Z Society. Now, the 7 Society, that's where the mystery is! They're also a service organization, but nobody knows how the society started or who the members are. It's said that membership is only revealed upon death. A special wreath is laid on the grave of a member."

"Several presidents of U.Va. have been members, but obviously they've passed now since we know who they were," said Aunt Leigh.

"How do you get to be a member of any of these societies? If no one knows who's in them, how do you ask to join? Or how would you believe you're really being asked to join? Is there some strange initiation ceremony?" asked Jason.

"Can you be in all three societies? I'd want to be in them all so I'd know everyone's secrets," said Tayleigh.

I thought about it for a minute and added, "I don't think I'd need to be in a club. I could pretend I was, and no one would know if my good deeds are because of the secret societies or not."

"All good questions, but I don't have the answers. We may have to do some research either online or in a library," replied Uncle TJ.

"There are so many books written about secret societies, including their practices, entry procedures, weird customs, and lots of other things. Of course, you'll never really know if the information you're reading is real unless you're in one of those societies. My favorite books to read are about the Knights Templar and the Illuminati," explained Aunt Leigh.

"Can we move this conversation to a restaurant? I'm so hungry!" I wailed.

"Italian anyone?" asked Uncle TJ.

We all responded with a chorus of "Yes!"

"We can stop at a bookstore over near the restaurant, and maybe we'll find a book about the secret societies at U.Va.," suggested Aunt Leigh. "That's a souvenir I'd like to buy."

4

Back in Michigan

"We're going to head downstairs for breakfast around eight o'clock, so you all can sleep in a little bit tomorrow. We'll leave straight from there for Poplar Forest," said Aunt Leigh.

"I hardly call that sleeping in!" whined Tayleigh. "That means I'll have to get up extra early to get any time in the bathroom."

"Thankfully this hotel room has two bathrooms and your uncle and I are quick in the morning," laughed Aunt Leigh.

"Here they are," announced Uncle TJ as we all crowded around him. Finally, our cell phones. I could text Allie and find out what had been going on back in Michigan. I felt like we'd been in Virginia forever already. "Jason, why don't you also upload some pictures and video to Facebook so everyone can see what we've been doing."

"Can I use your computer? It'll be faster," said Jason.

"Holler if you need us, but we're going to go watch some news in the bedroom so we can catch up on what's going on in the world," said Aunt Leigh.

"Hey, Bryant is online!" shouted Jason as Uncle TJ and Aunt Leigh were leaving the room. "I'm going to open a video chat with him so we can say hi."

We all crowded around the computer. It may not have been the popular thing for a college student to talk to his little siblings while he was in his dorm room, but Bryant never seemed to mind. We chatted with him most weeks, but sometimes we were all too busy.

"Hi from northern Virginia!" Bryant said as he waved to everyone once the connection came through. That was a little family joke. Once when Uncle TJ and Aunt Leigh were in Virginia, the guy who pretended to be Thomas Jefferson said Michigan was really northern Virginia. It turns out that it actually was—before it was Michigan and before we were the United States. We all saw the Mitchell Map hanging in their living room that shows what we now know as Michigan being part of Virginia.

"So should we call U of M the University of Northern Virginia instead?" asked Tayleigh laughing. "For real, though, I want to tell you all about U.Va. today. It's gorgeous!"

"Before everyone tells Bryant all about our trip so far, love from us, honey," said Aunt Leigh as she blew him a kiss.

Uncle TJ waved and added, "We wish you were here with us!" Uncle TJ then turned to us. "Okay, we'll let you guys talk now. Remember, no lazy kids in the morning. We expect you all to be ready to head downstairs at eight sharp! Good night."

"Okay, now I'm going to tell you all about U.Va.," continued Tayleigh.

"I'm the one who started the chat with Bryant," whined Jason. "I want to tell him about the Dome Room."

"Hey, Bry, while they're fighting, I have a question for you about when you came down here. Did you ever hear any voices that sounded kind of like Thomas Jefferson that would tell you facts about him? I know it sounds crazy, but I keep hearing things about Jefferson everywhere we go, but I seem to be the only one hearing them," I explained. As I was asking Bryant about this, I was silently congratulating myself for beating Jason. I outsmarted him at his own game. Instead of arguing with him about talking to Bryant first, I let him argue with Tayleigh. Yep, ingenious of me.

Bryant replied, "Sorry, Polly, never heard of such a thing. The only talking Jefferson I remember was the guy we met at Poplar Forest."

"Never mind. It's nothing," I blurted.

"Jason! Hey, Jase!" yelled Bryant. Jason stopped pushing at Tayleigh and turned back to the computer. "Now tell me about the Dome Room."

Jason started multitasking, uploading some video clips to Facebook while also telling Bryant a lot about the Monticello part of our trip. I uploaded a few pictures with my phone and started texting Allie. Tayleigh, while waiting to talk to Bryant, was texting Leo and Marli.

"Wow!" I shouted. "Allie said they got a weird late-spring snow today. Not lots of snow, but enough that she could stand outside and eat some snowflakes as they fell. It didn't stick to the ground though, so no snow wishes."

"Thank goodness," Tayleigh replied, and we both laughed.

I continued texting Allie about the weirdness going on with me. She, of all people, would believe me. She thought that Jason was playing a prank on me by playing clips from the Internet when I wasn't paying attention, which was a good idea except Jason's phone got taken away too. She asked if I wanted her to confirm any of the things I'd heard to make sure I wasn't just making them up, but I'd already basically done that by asking Uncle TJ and Aunt Leigh.

"Now I kind of wish we weren't in Virginia," said Tayleigh quietly, but it was loud enough that I heard her.

"Why? Aren't you having a great time?" I asked.

"Mostly. Marli needs me though. She and Alex broke up today. She said he kind of likes Cindy, and he didn't think it was fair to keep dating Marli. She said he was nice about it, but she didn't see it coming at all. I can't very well give her a hug from here."

"Maybe you can video chat with her for a while after we're all done talking to Bryant. It might help her to see you," I suggested.

"Great idea! I'm going to text her to go over to our house to get my computer. Then I'll text Mom to let her know Marli is walking over. Thanks, sis," smiled Tayleigh as she gave me a hug.

Oops! Mom and Dad! We hadn't talked to them yet. I realized we probably should video chat with them first. Then again, they didn't use the computer to video chat unless one of us started the program, so I didn't know if they could even figure out how to get it started on Tayleigh's Mac. "I'm going to call Mom and Dad if anyone wants to talk to them when I'm done," I announced.

"Tayleigh, your turn. You can tell Bryant about U.Va. now," said Jason. "I gotta talk to Scooter."

Isn't technology great? We were all uploading photos, texting, video chatting, and talking on the phone. How did people live before all of this technology? I couldn't even imagine my life back in the colonial days. I mean, there were definitely some interesting things about that time period, but there was also a lot missing.

The next thing I knew, I was sitting in one of the blue chairs in the yellow room they used as a dining room at Monticello. The man I kept seeing was sitting in the other chair in front of the fireplace.

"It takes a message many days to get to Monticello. I am always sending directions for my staff about cooking, farming, caring for the grapes, and other things when I am not here. Sometimes it could be a month before I know if they are following my directions. With thanks, I know Isaac is running the smithy the correct way, James is cooking well for everyone, and my daughter continues to manage it all."

The man looked out the window as I saw several people walk by, including a woman that I was certain was his daughter, Patsy.

"Mr. Jefferson, sir, may I please ask you a question?" I reverently said. He smiled at me, nodded, and . . . I was back in the hotel room. I just blinked, and Monticello, Jefferson, and everyone else were gone. I really had created a whole Polly World, but now Thomas Jefferson lived in it! I looked over at Tayleigh and Jason, who were both still busy doing their own things. I guessed I at least didn't talk out loud.

I texted Allie, asking her to look up who Isaac and James were at Monticello. She was fast on Google, or wherever she looked things up, because she texted back almost immediately. Sure enough, Isaac was a blacksmith, and James was a cook. She even said that James was trained in France. My life was just weird.

"You're going to be so jealous," Jason started chanting in a sing-song kind of way. "You're going to be so jealous!" He was dancing around the room, getting louder by the second.

"I know we said you guys could stay up late as long as you get up on time, but you need to keep it down," said Uncle TJ as he walked back into the living room. "You can talk to whomever you want, but you need to be respectful of other people in the rooms next to us."

"But, Uncle TJ, I just got the most exciting news!" shouted Jason. "Sorry, I didn't mean to say it that loudly," he whispered. "Anyway, Scooter just told me that the band is going to Disney World next year! We're going to be fundraising all summer long to help pay for the trip, but then we're going to be playing in some middle school competition at Disney. We won't march in the parade like the high school bands do, but it doesn't matter . . . we're going to Disney World!"

"I heard my favorite words," said Aunt Leigh from around the corner. We all knew how much Aunt Leigh loved Mickey Mouse. "Maybe I'll have to chaperone."

"Scooter said that they're looking for some chaperones. His parents can't take time off work to go though," explained Jason. "I doubt Mom could take time off of work either. Dad's schedule is a little easier, but I don't think he'll go if Mom doesn't go. Maybe you and Uncle TJ could chaperone."

"Maybe I could," said Bryant through the laptop. "When we took our trip to Mackinac Island with band, we had some prior band students serve as chaperones. Find out the dates of when it is. If my classes don't conflict with it, maybe I could go along."

"That would be awesome! I never get to see you any more, so we could hang out on the trip. You could be my guest in the trombone section," suggested Jason. "Now I'm getting excited about it!"

"That's still months away, Jase, and we have more fun things you need to focus on while we're in Virginia," Uncle TJ said. "I think all of you need to sign off and go to bed."

"Just a few more minutes, please," begged Tayleigh. "Marli just broke up with Alex, and she ran over to our house to get my laptop so we could video chat for a bit. Sorry, Bryant, but I'm going to say good-bye to you now."

"I see where I stand. Thanks for sharing, guys. Have a great time!" shouted Bryant as he disconnected.

"A few more minutes, but please do it quietly," conceded Uncle TJ.

Allie and I weren't going to video chat anyway, and I could quietly text all night long. Sometimes we stayed up texting past midnight, even on school nights. It was already close to midnight now. I still had to update Allie on a few more things before going to bed.

5

Poplar Forest

"How far is the drive to Poplar Forest?" It didn't matter because I had a great view out the window. There were little mountains, old country churches, and creeks. It was so spectacularly beautiful in Virginia.

"A little over an hour," replied Uncle TJ. "We should be there around ten."

Tayleigh started bouncing around in the backseat. "I totally forgot to tell you guys some things at breakfast! I didn't want to wake you up last night because it was really late when Morgan and Sabrina texted me—"

"I probably don't want to know just how late it was, do I?" interrupted Aunt Leigh.

Tayleigh snickered ".Probably not. Anyway, Morgan said that our high school dance team has been invited to submit a video to audition for a national dance competition. We have two weeks to create a dance that meets certain specifications, film it, and send it in. If we're one of the teams that make it through the first round, we'll be invited to Los Angeles for the national competition!"

My mind was racing as Tayleigh was explaining it. Tay and I went to dance classes outside of school, but I wasn't on a dance team at school because we didn't have it in the middle school. "That's so amazing, Tay! I wish it was the dance studio instead, so I could be part of it," I complained.

"If we make it, maybe we'll be invited back in the future. Who knows, maybe it'll happen when you're in high school too," offered Tayleigh.

"I have to make the dance team first," I sighed.

"You're a Vesper," stated Jason. "Of course you'll make it." I savored his compliment. They didn't happen too often.

"That is exciting, Tayleigh. A team trip to LA would be very expensive though. Any more details on the trip or what song and moves you have to do?" asked Aunt Leigh.

"Morgan did say we shouldn't get our hopes up too much for LA because the coach said we might not be able to afford to go. I guess it would be cool just to know we were good enough to get there, even if we can't go. She also said the coach asked us each to come to practice next week and share our top three favorite dance moves. Then we'll see if any of those moves meet the requirements. She wants us all involved in the planning of the dance. I'm going to be thinking about moves the rest of this trip!"

Uncle TJ looked in the rearview mirror at Tayleigh and said, "I hope you'll focus on the trip as well. I'd hate for you to miss out on the fun we still have planned because you're dwelling too much on dance. You can think about moves the entire ride home on Sunday."

"I'll help too. I can tell you some of my favorite moves I've seen you guys do, and maybe you'll get some ideas that way too," I suggested. "I really liked two of the dances you guys did during basketball season, and I remember almost all the steps."

"Thanks. That's not all of the exciting news though! Sabrina also texted me about the spring concert. She said Ms. Planter wants to spice up the concert a bit, so we're not going to do our typical choir concert. We're going to do popular songs and maybe some mash-ups. This is going to be great! I love singing anyway, but it'll be a lot more fun to be singing songs we like with cool dance moves. I bet I can share some ideas for our dance steps there too," said Tayleigh as she started moving her arms in small motions.

"With all of your exciting news, sounds like you were probably up most of the night," said Aunt Leigh. "I just hope you don't fall asleep on us today."

"Give me the caffeine, and I'm ready to go," replied Tay with a yawn. We all laughed.

"Scooter told me about baseball practice," added Jason. "I guess I didn't miss anything there. The news about the band trip is way exciting though. I was thinking about it some more, and it would be awesome if you guys could chaperone. I mean, I think I need to ask Mom and Dad first, but . . ."

Aunt Leigh turned around, looking at Jason. "We totally understand. Of course you'll want to ask your parents first. If that doesn't work out, we'd be happy to look at our work schedules and see. You know I always love to go to Disney. Although, if Bryant wants to chaperone, we don't want to take any spot away from him either. There's plenty of time to think about it, so don't worry. It'll all work out."

"I feel like I didn't talk to the right people last night. Allie and I talked a lot, but mostly about this trip. I don't have any gossip to share from home. She even helped look up a few facts about Jefferson for me, like the fact that the Louisiana Purchase doubled the size of the United States, cost about fifteen million dollars, and was authorized by President Jefferson."

"At least one of you is here in the present and really focused on the trip," said Uncle TJ. "Allie found accurate information, too. That was a bold move by Jefferson, and it helped make the United States what it is today."

"There are many things I like about Jefferson, but one of my favorite things is a quote from a letter he wrote to John Adams," explained Aunt Leigh. "The quote said 'I cannot live without books.' You all know how much I read, so I appreciate that sentiment very much. You know, I think Jefferson actually read more than I do!"

"Impossible!" shouted Tayleigh with dramatic flair. "You're always reading a book or stopping at the library or wandering through a book store. Okay, so maybe not on this trip, but I think we're a little busy."

"She did read part of a book on her iPad last night while you were all video chatting and texting," laughed Uncle TJ.

"Isn't that quote on your bracelet?" I asked.

"Yes," acknowledged Aunt Leigh. "That's Jefferson's handwriting. I bought it at Poplar Forest."

"You guys need to start thinking a little bit about James Madison too. If you remember, when we're at Poplar Forest, we're going to see a conversation between Presidents Jefferson and Madison. They're going to be acting like it's 1811, so it will be in the middle of Madison's first term as president," explained Uncle TJ.

"I'm glad we went to Montpelier yesterday then," reflected Jason. "This way I know some things about him. I also know that his wife didn't just make donuts."

"You may even have an opportunity to ask a question during the conversation. Just remember, these gentlemen will stay in character and only answer questions that are relevant from 1811 or before," continued Uncle TJ.

"I can't ask Jefferson about his retirement at Monticello or freeing some slaves upon his death?" I asked. Some of the most interesting things about him were when he wasn't in the spotlight as much.

"I long for my own retirement so strongly, but the country has other plans for me as I continue to serve my public duty. My greatest wish is to retire and spend my days at Monticello as a farmer."

"Yes, that's exactly what I was wondering," I replied to Uncle TJ.

"Wondering about what?" Uncle TJ asked. "Were you even listening to what I said? I was explaining again that you have to pretend that we're all in 1811, and you must ask questions related to that."

"I was just thinking that I understand why Jefferson would want to retire and farm at Monticello" I said quietly. Man, Polly World struck again.

"That is true. In fact, I think he even wrote something about that in a letter to James Monroe, who wasn't only a president but also a good friend of Jefferson's," clarified Uncle TJ.

"Did Allie text that to you last night?" asked Aunt Leigh. "I have a feeling we're going to be hearing many interesting facts from Allie through you."

"Yep, you guessed it. Just thought I'd try to look smart," I laughed weakly. Or Polly World was invading my real life too much and I was going crazy. Or I had a brain tumor. Or I ate something strange. Had I eaten anything different from anyone else? Or I hadn't gotten enough sleep. *No, it's true; I'm just losing my mind . . .*

—⟆⟆⟆—

"Wake up, Polly!" yelled Jason as he shook my shoulders. "You were snoring! I don't know how you can fall asleep so fast. You were talking one minute, and then you were zonked. Wake up! We're here!"

I didn't realize that I'd fallen asleep. I thought I was just daydreaming some more. Guess it was actual dreaming. I looked out the window and saw that we were pulling into a long, wooded drive that had a

Poplar Forest sign at the entrance. I could almost imagine that we were in a horse and buggy heading up that dirt and stone trail to visit Mr. Jefferson while he was there on vacation.

"I like to retreat to Poplar Forest to escape the responsibilities of my mountain top home. While I love having people visit Monticello, they stay for extended visits because I do feel it is rude to turn them out. My granddaughters often visit Poplar Forest with me, but I rarely have other visitors."

"Is that the guy who acts like Jefferson?" I asked, pointing into the woods at the man dressed in what I imagined was colonial gardening gear. He had something in his hand he was writing on as he was looking at some flowers. What a wonderful way to welcome us to Poplar Forest!

"I can't see him from here," responded Uncle TJ. "I'd expect he's up closer to the house."

Of course, no one was there. My imagination had totally taken over. I needed to divert attention before they locked me up in the loony bin! "Jefferson really did come here to get away from everything, didn't he?"

"Literally," said Tayleigh. "He even escaped being under attack once and came here."

Uncle TJ nodded. "This was his vacation home, although I'm not even sure the word vacation was around then. He still had lots of work to do when he was here like managing his staff, writing letters with directions back to Monticello, overseeing the farming, and reading books, but it was a place of rest and rejuvenation for him. With such a small house compared to Monticello, he didn't have as many people living in the house with him."

"I see it!" said Jason. I could just barely see the top of his house above some trees or bushes, but he was right. He had his iPod out and handed it to me. "I want to introduce this one." I quickly changed seats with him so I could shoot his head with the road to Poplar Forest in the background. "Welcome to Poplar Forest, Jefferson's famous octagonal home. Well, it's not so famous because it was like his hiding place . . . his secret lair . . . his Batcave. He would stay here for a while when he needed a break from business at home or as president."

"Batcave . . . I love it!" shouted Uncle TJ after Jason finished.

We drove past the house to a parking lot and went to the visitor's center to get our tour tickets. As we walked into the visitor's center, a couple of ladies called out my aunt and uncle's names and came over to give them hugs. I knew they went there a lot, but I was surprised that any staff members would remember their names. One of the women turned to us and said, "Welcome back, Tayleigh, and you two must be Polly and Jason." Wow, she even knew our names! "I think you're all going to have a wonderful time here today. There are some archeologists working, so you can see firsthand how we're able to learn so much about Mr. Jefferson. Of course you'll also enjoy your special lunch before the conversation."

"I need this T-shirt," called Tayleigh, obviously already shopping.

"We'll have time later to look around the gift shop, but let's join the tour that's just getting ready to start," suggested Aunt Leigh.

Uncle TJ said, "Remember to look for commonalities between Poplar Forest and Monticello. I think you'll notice architectural similarities as well as other familiarities about the lay of the land."

"Didn't that lady mention lunch? When is lunch?" asked Jason.

"It's only ten o'clock! Simmer down," joked Uncle TJ. "We're going on the tour first, and then we'll walk around the rest of Poplar Forest a little bit. Lunch will get here soon enough."

A tour guide came out of a little building with some other people. "That's our tour. Come on guys," motioned Aunt Leigh.

Poplar Forest, President Jefferson's retreat home.

"Ah, here's our Michigan crew," said the tour guide. "Welcome back. Hi, kids, my name is Donna. Now, as I was saying, you'll notice how the backyard is dug down deeper. This was done to allow the basement of the house to be built, and you'll see that it also provides the illusion of a larger backyard when you stand on the portico. Jefferson offered to pay any of his slaves extra to dig out that area on their own time, but only one slave took him up on it. The extra dirt created the mounds on either side of the house, again creating that symmetry that Jefferson is so well known for . . ."

Wow, that was so much work for one person to do, especially after working the entire day out in the fields already. I couldn't ever do it. It must have taken years. I wondered if that slave earned enough money to buy his freedom. Could he even do that? Maybe he buried some secrets in the mounds of dirt. I liked the trees that were on those dirt mounds. It was kind of like a garden of trees. Maybe we can run up to the top later and take some pictures.

"Polly!" yelled Jason. They were a lot closer to the house than I was. I hurried and joined them as we walked through an opening in the bushes to get to the front door. Jason got out the iPod to film some of Donna's introduction to the house and then me walking up to the front door.

"No filming or photography inside the house," said Donna as we were entering the house.

We walked through the house from room to room. What an unusual house with every room, except the dining room, in the shape of an octagon. Jefferson had his bed in the middle of the room in an alcove type configuration again, so maybe one side was his bedroom and one side was his office like at Monticello. The weird thing there was that there was no furniture or pictures on the wall. Monticello was like someone was living in it, and this house was like someone was building it. It was kind of hard to imagine what everything would look like with someone living in it.

"Ms. Donna, why aren't there any pictures on the walls?" I asked.

"I'll talk more about that in the last room, but basically we decided to highlight the restoration process of Poplar Forest. There are still discussions going on about whether to furnish the house with Jeffersonian era pieces once the restoration is complete. Now, if anyone would like to try sitting in Jefferson's favorite chair, the Campeche chair, please follow me into the next room."

"I love this sling-back chair from the Campeche province in Mexico. It took me many years to finally purchase such a chair of my own, and then I had a copy of it built at Monticello so I can have one with me everywhere."

"President Jefferson had his own slaves and artisans figure out how to make the chair because he loved it so much," I said, not realizing how loudly I'd spoken.

"You're absolutely right. In fact, it was John Hemings who made Jefferson's beloved chair," continued Donna.

"Not fair," whispered Jason. "I knew that too. We've sat in Uncle TJ's Campeche chair enough. You just had to show off though."

That's really not what I was doing. I honestly didn't realize I'd spoken loudly enough for anyone to hear. Oh well, score one for Polly over Jason . . . I could deal with that.

We walked into the next room, which was exactly the same as Jefferson's bedroom on the other side of the house. "If you look out the window, you'll see the wing of offices that we've recently reconstructed. We'll walk out there after the tour, but you can see that anyone inside the house could easily take a stroll by going out this door," explained Donna.

In the final room, Donna showed us how the artisans restoring Poplar Forest had to build the walls back layer by layer. Not only did it take the slaves and other people forever to build Poplar Forest and the surrounding grounds, it's taking the people restoring it just as long. I never could be so patient. We then followed Donna back out the front door as she led us up the stairs to the rooftop over the wing of offices. "After you've walked around here, please walk around to the back of the house so you can go into the kitchen and other structures underneath, as well as the basement of the house," said Donna as she turned to us. "And we'll see your family under the tent in a little while."

We walked past the tent on the way around the house. "We're eating there?" asked Tayleigh.

"Yes, they've invited us to join a luncheon with the men participating in the conversation. Of course Phil Parker, better known as Thomas Jefferson, will be there. The gentleman portraying James Madison will also be there," explained Uncle TJ. "I know I don't need to say this, but don't forget to use your manners while we're at lunch."

"Duh," retorted Jason. "We're always wonderful."

The ground floor, underneath the part of Poplar Forest we toured, was full of details about the Jefferson era. We saw the cellar, a rat's nest, the kitchen, and many little things they'd found while excavating the grounds. It was kind of neat to think that the little fork in the display could be the one that Jefferson used.

"No way!" screeched Jason. No one yelled at him, so I guess it was okay that he was a little noisy down there. "I found an indoor privy! I thought the one by the mound of dirt was the only toilet here."

"Jefferson did have an indoor privy down the stairs below his bedroom. You can see it wasn't big at all. It probably was just a chamber pot that was emptied for him. It's not like there was indoor plumbing," explained Aunt Leigh. "You didn't get to see the indoor privy at Monticello, but there was one."

"I didn't see anywhere there could be a bathroom there. I would have noticed," retorted Jason.

"There were a few doors that we didn't get to open," said Uncle TJ. "You probably didn't notice them because they closed us into each room as we went through the tour. There's a little closet off Jefferson's bedroom where there's an indoor privy too."

"Did he have the first indoor toilets in America?" I asked.

"I don't know," replied Uncle TJ. "We'll have to ask about that." Had Uncle TJ just said he didn't know the answer? I couldn't believe I stumped him! He knew everything about Thomas Jefferson. I got out my camera and quickly snapped a picture of my uncle.

"What was that for? I wasn't ready," laughed Uncle TJ as he struck a silly pose.

"I have to always remember the moment you said that you didn't know something!" I replied. Jason and Tayleigh clapped for me, and Aunt Leigh cracked up.

"I think we need to come back to the present day and head up to lunch," suggested Aunt Leigh. "No privy talk up there, okay?"

"I'm going to be too busy shoveling food in my mouth. Don't worry," responded Jason.

We walked around to the tent that was near the front entrance of Poplar Forest. There were older people there, and everyone was so dressed up. Now I understood why Aunt Leigh made us wear better clothes that day. We weren't dressed in our church clothes, but the rule was no T-shirts, shorts, or sneakers.

"Most of the people here are either board members for Poplar Forest or have been involved for a long time with the restoration process," whispered Aunt Leigh. "Please be polite, even if you don't like some of the food. If you're still hungry, we've got some snacks in the car you can eat before we go into the conversation."

"I became fond enough of French cuisine that I had my personal cook trained in France. I also discovered a personal taste for vanilla bean ice cream in France and often have it prepared since my return home."

I noticed the man who must be Phil Parker with a bowl of ice cream in his hands. I supposed if you're playing Thomas Jefferson, you can eat your ice cream first. "Maybe we'll have vanilla ice cream because Jefferson liked that so much," I said.

"Ah yes, just one more thing that Jefferson and I have in common," sighed Uncle TJ. He was always joking about how he and Jefferson shared the same soul. I smiled at him and noticed another Thomas Jefferson standing a ways behind Uncle TJ. He was with another colonial man and a few other people. He was obviously explaining something about the house because he was pointing over that way. I quickly looked back to where Mr. Jefferson had been eating ice cream, but there wasn't anyone there. There was no way he could have moved that fast. Was it Mr. Jefferson's ghost eating ice cream? I wondered if anyone has researched Jefferson's ghost. Maybe he haunted those places.

—◦◦◦—

Lunch was extremely fancy. Everyone was friendly, and most people seemed to know who we were. I guess we kind of stood out because we were the only kids there. We sat with a couple from Philadelphia who loved Jefferson almost as much as Uncle TJ and Aunt Leigh did. I was happy to see the dessert was vanilla ice cream with some fresh berries on it.

"Here's our opportunity to have your picture taken with the presidents," said Aunt Leigh as she motioned for everyone to follow her. "I see Phil over there getting ready to head to the conversation. He'll be busy during and after the show, so now is the best time for us to say hi and get in a quick photo." She sure did take a ton of pictures.

"Mr. Madison, let me introduce you to my friends from northern Virginia," said President Jefferson as we walked up to him. "This is TJ and Leigh, and I believe these are their nieces and nephew."

"What an honor to meet your family," said President Madison. "I've heard that you make the long journey often to visit Mr. Jefferson."

I was feeling like the Patriot Princess again. It was so awesome that everyone knew who we were. It was like we were the superstars, when really it was the presidents who were the stars there. "It's an honor to meet both of you," I said as I curtsied. We did a move that was like a curtsy in dance before, so I just did that. Tayleigh copied me, and Jason bowed. While I was being nice, I wanted to grab Mr. Parker's shoulders, shake him, and ask him why I kept hearing his voice everywhere! It was kind of comforting, for a change, that everyone else could hear him now too.

"And what polite children they are," continued President Madison.

"We're all looking forward to hearing both of you talk," said Uncle TJ. "We always have such a good time on our trip, and it's great that the kids were able to come along this time."

"Remember to think about what questions you may have for us," offered President Jefferson. "Mr. Madison and I will talk for a time, but we love to take questions from our friends."

There was some more talk among the adults, but I didn't pay too close attention to it. I smiled when Aunt Leigh took our picture with the presidents, and then we headed back over to the gift shop for a little shopping before the show. It was funny how no one called it a show. Everyone called it "the conversation." I mean, if the men were performing as historical characters, wasn't it a show or play? It was totally freaking me out to hear President Jefferson speak in person. His voice was definitely the voice I'd been hearing the last few days. I didn't care how crazy Aunt Leigh and Uncle TJ thought I was, I had to talk with them about this later. If someone was playing a joke on me, I needed to know. If I was going crazy, I needed to know that too.

As we walked into the tent where the conversation was going to happen, we met up with some of Aunt Leigh and Uncle TJ's friends from Virginia, the Andersons, to sit with them. Jason got out the iPod to film some of the conversation, but Uncle TJ made him put it away.

At least he filmed a little bit when we talked to the presidents outside. The presidents started talking, and everyone was laughing along with their jokes. Surprisingly, it was interesting. I thought I'd get bored just listening to a conversation between two people, but they were entertaining. They talked about everything from family to farming to being president to visiting each other. They also talked a lot about Dolley Madison, which was cool, because I thought she was impressive when we visited Montpelier. I decided Jefferson and Madison had good views about women because Jefferson made sure his daughters went to school and Madison married a very smart wife. Many men during that time felt that women should cook in the kitchen and that was about it.

"Everyone should be educated to preserve liberty."

Exactly what I was thinking! Well, maybe not the liberty part, and I wasn't sure I quite understood that. I looked up at President Jefferson to nod, but he was sitting down watching President Madison speak. Ugh! It was that voice in my head again. That's it! I'm going to ask them a question about that and see if they can explain it to me. Soon enough, it was time for questions, so I shot my hand up. The Andersons' son asked the first question, and then I got to ask the next one.

"I know you both believed in education for all people, not just the boys," I started, "but I think I heard Mr. Jefferson say something about education helps preserve liberty. I don't really understand that. Can you please explain more?"

"Excellent question, young lady," replied President Jefferson. "My colleague and I are avid enthusiasts of education. We both have taken our own education as far as it could go formally and continue to be educated through readings, discussions, and experiences. I have provided schooling and tutoring for my children and grandchildren, finding that only through education can people understand the world. In order to be able to govern ourselves with any semblance of democracy, we have to ensure that education is a top priority. That brings me to your question. Many people do not understand liberty or what our liberty brings to us. We, Mr. Madison, myself, and many others, have fought to ensure liberty for our generation and those who come after us. However, if people do not understand the ancient struggle for liberty or what liberty means, they may lose it. Therefore, we must continue to educate everyone on the tenets of our great struggle for liberty and the principles of freedom upon which our nation was founded."

President Madison continued, "Which is exactly why Mr. Jefferson here, along with other colleagues of mine, encouraged the addition of the Bill of Rights to our Constitution. We wanted to ensure that various liberties would be guaranteed to future generations like the right to free speech or the right to practice religion."

The audience burst into applause, and Mr. Jefferson nodded at me appreciatively. I guess I asked a pretty good question. Maybe the voice in my head wasn't such a bad thing. A few more questions were asked, and then the discussion was over. It went by so quickly, and I was paying attention.

When everyone was standing up to shake hands with the presidents, Uncle TJ gave me a big hug. "Liberty is one of my favorite things to talk about! What made you think to ask that question?"

"It was just floating around in my head," I said with my head tilted to the ground. "I must have heard something about that at one of the places we've been." I was thinking that I should text Allie to have her look up the actual phrase I heard to see if it really was a Jefferson quote. I did that quietly as we waited in the receiving line. She immediately texted back. Turns out that a phrase very similar to that was part of the display at the Jefferson Memorial in Washington, DC. Yet I'd never been to DC. She couldn't find where Jefferson originally said that, but she said there were lots of links that explained his views on it.

"Last chance to buy anything in the bookstore," called Aunt Leigh. "We're going to go out to dinner with the Andersons and then decide what we want to do next."

"We have choices?" asked Jason.

"You know how they love to force us to make choices," laughed Tayleigh. It was kind of a joke that we all had a hard time making decisions. Sometimes one of us wanted to do something, and we'd complain and whine until we did it or got in trouble. But, for the most part, we were just along on this trip to spend some time with our aunt and uncle. Plus, we got to miss a few days of school!

"So what are our choices?" I asked. I hoped one of the choices was to go back to the pool at the hotel. It was warmer than I thought it would be, and it would have felt so good right then to be in the pool.

"We've got one more full day of our trip, and then we'll be driving home the last day. So, we need to figure out what we want to do tomorrow. There are so many things to do and see in and around Virginia, but we decided to leave the last day up to you three. Why don't you lay out the options, Leigh?" said Uncle TJ.

"I vote that we drive south and hang out at Disney World for a day!" shouted Jason.

"While I'd love that, it's a little out of our way," laughed Aunt Leigh. "We were thinking of some other historical locales. One option would be to drive around this part of Virginia some more to see the D-Day Memorial, the Natural Bridge, and some other places along the way. Another option is to drive over to Colonial Williamsburg for the day tomorrow to see the town and catch a few short shows. Yet another option could be to stop in Richmond, Virginia's capitol, to tour several buildings there. Finally, a day in Washington, DC at some of the memorials or Smithsonian Museums could be in the plans. We realize that any one of these days could be a full vacation in itself, so we'll be cramming a lot into one day no matter which one you pick. Or, I suppose, you may just choose to relax a day to go swimming, shopping, and sleep in. The choice is all yours."

"Sleep and shop!" yelled Tayleigh. Of course that was what she'd want to do. Like she actually had any money left to spend. I doubted it.

"I want to go to DC," offered Jason. "That's like the headquarters for the country."

"Maybe we should explore more around here," I said. "It's not like we're going to come back here soon, and I don't want to miss anything." While our aunt and uncle visited Virginia a lot, we certainly didn't. I wanted to do everything they mentioned, but I knew there wasn't enough time. Although, maybe if we went to Colonial Williamsburg or Washington, DC, I'd get some more answers about the voice I kept hearing. I thought maybe the voice would stop once I met President Jefferson, but it didn't. "I changed my mind. Maybe we should go to Colonial Williamsburg. Isn't that where Mr. Parker works full-time as President Jefferson?"

"We just met him," whined Jason. "Besides, he's here, not there."

"He'll probably be back at work in Williamsburg tomorrow," said Uncle TJ. "He may have a performance or two to give then, so it's possible we'd see him there. There's a lot more to do at Williamsburg other than just see President Jefferson, but that's why we wanted your opinions on this. There are so many things we love to do, and we want to share it all with you."

"Okay, we'll take next week off of school. You've convinced us," sighed Tayleigh like it was something so painful to do. We cracked up. That would be so nice, though. I couldn't believe our trip was going so quickly!

"We could go see one of the performances while at Colonial Williamsburg. They have some fun, interactive ones that we've done before like learning how to march. There's also one where the audience is part of the jury to decide if someone is guilty of being a witch. Oh, there's one I've always wanted to do," continued Aunt Leigh. "It's a ghost tour of Williamsburg by night. Although, Polly might be too scared."

"I would not!" I emphatically denied. "I like to read mysteries. I just don't like to watch a lot of scary movies. It's probably not that scary . . . is it?" Maybe they'd share some information about Jefferson's ghost, and then I'd know I wasn't completely crazy. Or, at least I could ask some questions about how to know when you're seeing a ghost.

"I want to do that. It would be great to include some ghost stories of colonial days in our video for class," confirmed Jason.

Tayleigh added, "I've never been there either, so I'm game. Is there shopping?"

"There are many little shops there, and my favorite candy store anywhere," mentioned Uncle TJ.

"Sold! Let's go to Colonial Williamsburg!" decided Jason.

"Williamsburg it is," announced Uncle TJ. "We'll drive over there after dinner tonight so we can sleep in a little bit before heading in to see the Governor's Palace. Leigh, we'll need to find a hotel for tonight."

Aunt Leigh nodded, but she was already ahead of the game. She was on her phone talking to some reservation agent. "Got it. We'll all be crammed into one room on this short of notice, but there's a pool so you guys can go swimming later tonight if you want."

"Now let's go find the Andersons so we can head out to dinner. I think Jason is withering away to nothing," said Uncle TJ.

"You're right! I'm starving!" lamented Jason. Some things never change.

～ **6** ～

Colonial Williamsburg

"Did you know that the Wren Building at the College of William &
Mary is the oldest academic college building in the whole country that
has been continuously used since the days of Thomas Jefferson and
well before?" asked Jason as we were walking from the visitor's center
into Colonial Williamsburg.

"We were all in the room when you were video chatting with
Bryant when he told us that!" I reminded him. He was a little jealous
that I kept knowing things about Jefferson, and he still didn't believe
how I knew those things. He asked Bryant to look up some facts about
Williamsburg to share with us, but he should have done that a little
more discreetly. It was a little hard to hide anything going on from the
rest of us when we were all staying in the same small hotel room.

Jason muttered, "Well, I didn't know for sure if you were paying
attention."

"I have bad news for everyone," started Uncle TJ. "As we walk across
this bridge and read the plaques on the ground, you'll see we're going
back into time. You're going to feel like you really are going back in
time . . . not only because of the buildings and the interpreters dressed
in period attire, but because your cell phones aren't going to work."

"What? They're blocking our cell phones?" complained Tayleigh.
"I already don't like it here."

Aunt Leigh replied, "Not exactly. For some reason, and maybe it's on purpose, cell phones just don't work well in Colonial Williamsburg. So, don't bother trying to text because it's not going to work."

"Marli still needs me today. She's really upset about Alex," shared Tayleigh. "I also wanted to text Leo some pictures of what we're doing."

"Yeah, Allie was going to text me some places we should visit today," I added.

"Scooter was just going to tell me . . . well . . . probably nothing important, but now he's going to think I'm ignoring him," Jason lamented.

"Quickly text everyone and tell them you're traveling back in time," suggested Uncle TJ. "They may think you're crazy, but it's kind of true."

"Allie just replied that we do have to go to the College of William & Mary because Thomas Jefferson attended there as a student," I passed on to the group.

"Hello! Didn't I already suggest that?" shouted Jason, a little too loudly.

"Yes, yes, calm down," said Aunt Leigh. "We're definitely making a stop at the college, at least the historic area of the college, including the Wren Building. Now, phones away or I'll put them in the backpack. Let's finish reading these stepping stones and go back in time."

"My days at Williamsburg were some of the most thought-provoking days of my life. Studying with William Small and George Wythe, listening to the exciting ideas of Patrick Henry, and starting to practice law helped shape who I am as a person, lawyer, and politician."

"How long did Thomas Jefferson live here?" I asked. "I thought he just went to college here, but I also know he was a real lawyer when he lived here."

"That he was," agreed Uncle TJ. "You have to remember, though, that in those days people didn't go to law school for so long. You could become a lawyer simply by reading law books and taking a law test. Jefferson was also very young when he started college. I think he was maybe sixteen years old. I'm not sure how long he lived here, so we'll have to look for that information today."

"Did Uncle TJ just admit he doesn't know something about Jefferson again?" questioned Tayleigh, feigning to be in shock. "I'm not used to hearing so many 'I don't knows' from Uncle TJ."

"Okay, you can all have a little laugh at your uncle's expense. Now, come on, let's go explore," suggested Aunt Leigh. "That guy over there looks like he wants to tell us a story about the gardens."

We walked all over Colonial Williamsburg. It really wasn't that big of a city, but it was practically the center of our country for a while. So many important decisions about our country were made there. So many famous people lived there, and all at the same time! Battle Creek is even bigger than Williamsburg, so it was crazy for such a small place to be so important. Jason liked the Governor's Palace. He kept saying he should live in a mansion that big. Tayleigh's favorite part was the old Capitol. We even got to watch a mock trial go on there. I think my favorite place was the Bruton Parish Church because it didn't look like any other church I'd ever been in. The graveyard outside of the church was amazing, and people still use the church today.

Replica of the Capitol at Colonial Williamsburg.

We had walked by the George Wythe house earlier, but it was closed. After leaving the church, we saw the flag up by the Wythe house, which meant it was now open.

"Can we go into the Wythe house now?" I begged. "He was one of Jefferson's mentors, and I think Jefferson even stayed with him. I want to see how he lived while he was here."

"You're getting into this, aren't you?" questioned Aunt Leigh. "It's exciting for me to see all of this through all of your eyes. It's like seeing things again for the first time."

"You'll get to see it all a second, third, and fourth time, too, when our video is ready," joked Jason. He was filming down Duke of Gloucester Street, or DOG Street as the locals called it.

"Can I just go over to Starbucks and wait for you guys? I'm bored and want some hot cocoa," complained Tayleigh.

"Seriously? You've never been here before and now you want to skip things? No, you're coming in with us," said Uncle TJ. He looked very disappointed that Tayleigh didn't want to go with us.

"TJ, let her go. I'd rather she go relax for a little bit and find a better mood to be in the rest of the day than go to the Wythe house and moan the whole time," said Aunt Leigh.

"Fine," agreed Uncle TJ. "Stay in the bookstore though. We'll let you know when we're done." Tayleigh walked down the street, heading to the bookstore. She really hadn't been in a good mood all morning. She hadn't been in a bad mood either. Guess it was just one of those teen things.

We rushed over and made it with the group. We toured the grounds and gardens around the Wythe house before going inside. It was a large brick house, bigger than most of the houses we'd seen around Williamsburg.

"I was fortunate to study under Mr. Wythe, who later became the first law professor in America. I also had the opportunity to work with Mr. Wythe in revising the laws of Virginia."

I whispered to Uncle TJ, "Did you know that George Wythe was America's first law professor?"

"I'd forgotten that fact," he admitted. "Was that on one of the plaques on the wall?"

"You don't want to know. It was that weird voice again," I mumbled to myself as I walked away from Uncle TJ. Even though the voice was making me feel alone, it was wonderful to know some things that even Uncle TJ didn't know. I couldn't even enjoy feeling smart because then I'd have to tell everyone that I really was hearing that voice. They'd pretty much decided I was reading things, texting Allie, or overhearing other conversations. I hadn't mentioned the voice in a while. Maybe I should tell them all what's been going on. Maybe they can help me. It would be great if they could hear the voice.

"You're right, Polly, that was cool to see where Jefferson could have stayed when he visited, although he didn't live here. I just wish I could have filmed it. I guess I'll film some of the outside of the house to show how different this place is from Poplar Forest or Monticello," commented Jason.

The tour guide pointed out where Jefferson might have slept. I totally missed it. I was daydreaming about the voice. It was the first time that thinking about the voice caused me to miss something. What a bummer.

"I know we ate a late breakfast, but I'm starving. Can we find someplace to eat?" pleaded Jason.

"It is almost three o'clock. I agree with Jase, it's time for some food. I'll text Tayleigh so she can meet outside the bookstore as we walk by, and then we can find a place in Merchant's Square to eat and head on to the College of William & Mary after our meal," concurred Aunt Leigh.

Jason glared at Uncle TJ. "Wait! I thought you said our phones wouldn't work here. Was that a lie so we wouldn't try to use them?"

"Not a lie at all, calm down. They don't work in the old part of the city, but we're close enough to the college now, so they do work here," explained Uncle TJ. "Hey, Leigh, remember that place we ate before that had the strange sandwich?"

"There are two excellent restaurants that I love here," reminisced Aunt Leigh. "The Trellis is the place you're talking about, TJ. We had that sandwich that was toasted cinnamon raisin bread with sliced apples, peanut butter, and bacon."

"Ewwww!" I gasped. "That sounds horrible."

"We thought it sounded strange too, but it was surprisingly good. In fact, we make that sandwich at home often now too," explained Uncle TJ.

"There's also Aroma's. That's the coffeehouse that had the most amazing grilled cheese sandwich I've ever had," continued Aunt Leigh.

"Right. I remember that place too. Aroma's probably would be better for our gang. I remember the Trellis being a little fancier," suggested Uncle TJ.

"Food is good wherever there are mass quantities of food," laughed Jason. "There's Tayleigh. Hey, we're over here!" He was waving like a maniac. I think he got everyone's attention on the street. Tayleigh shuffled over to join us.

"You look much happier now," commented Uncle TJ.

"Quality texting time with Leo and Marli can do that," smiled Tayleigh. "I feel better knowing that Marli is doing okay. She's really bumming, but she's not a total wreck."

"Glad to hear that," said Aunt Leigh. "Aroma's it is. Follow me. It's not on DOG Street, but it's close."

Aunt Leigh was right; it was the best grilled cheese sandwich I'd ever had. It had three kinds of cheese, tomatoes, lettuce, and mayonnaise on it. I loved it! They had some amazing desserts that we all shared. It's probably a good thing we went at an odd time because the cafe wasn't that big, and Aunt Leigh said it got really crowded in there with lines going out the door. I wished Battle Creek had a restaurant like that. Maybe I could get Tayleigh to say that out loud in case any of her snow wish was still working. I decided I would love to work there someday. Who knows, maybe I'll go to the College of William & Mary and work at Aroma's. There, now I have my future all planned out. I could study colonial history. Wouldn't Uncle TJ just love that?

"That's the College of William & Mary just across the street," said Uncle TJ. "We'll go walk around the historic part of the college. They offer tours there."

"I want to see where the students live," said Tayleigh. "I think you can tell a lot from a campus by the dorms."

"You just want to see how big the rooms are to see if they're bigger than Bryant's room," said Jason.

"Okay, maybe you're right. I do want to find a good college, but I also want to live in comfort," explained Tayleigh.

Aunt Leigh chuckled. "You may think that's important now, but as you get closer to really deciding on what college to go to, you won't be thinking about the dorms. You'll be more focused on what college has the type of programs you're interested in and if you can afford to go there."

"I plan to get scholarships, so money won't be an issue," retorted Tayleigh.

"Admirable plan," agreed Uncle TJ. "You just need to make sure your grades are top notch so you can make that plan a reality."

"Look ahead," directed Aunt Leigh. "There's the Wren Building that Jason was talking about when we were at the visitor's center. That's where the tour begins, so let's go inside."

The tour guide was a college student, so it was interesting hearing her perspective on the building. The final room we went into was some type of classroom. The tour guide said Thomas Jefferson sat in there for some of his classes. We got to sit in the student seats, and the guide stood where the professor would stand, telling us more about Jefferson's time as a student there.

A man was standing near the fireplace, looking thoughtfully around the room. He really did look like Thomas Jefferson. As he walked toward a seat, he appeared to get younger and younger until he was just a teenager. I was seeing things! No way this was happening! I hit Jason lightly on his arm and pointed over at the man.

"I lived in this building for a short time as a student here. This is the room in which I learned much about mathematics and moral philosophy from William Small."

"Ouch! Stop that!" Jason yelled. He knew I didn't hurt him; he just wanted to get me in trouble.

"Both of you cut it out right now," warned Uncle TJ. "The tour isn't over. Show some respect to our guide." Uncle TJ rarely got mad at us, so I felt horrible. I wasn't trying to cause any problems. I just wanted someone else to see the ghost that kept following me. I hung my head down. Jason didn't seem to care.

"Any questions about our tour?" asked the student.

I slowly raised my hand and asked, "I didn't see any dorm rooms in this building, but I thought that Jefferson lived here when he was a student."

"You're right, he did. The building wasn't used in the same way then, so there were some rooms that were set up like dorms. You have to remember that in those days, too, rooms had multiple uses. A room that was a classroom in the morning might have been a cafeteria at meals and a recreational hall in the evening. People were very good at making multiple uses of space," the tour guide explained.

Uncle TJ put his arm around me and whispered, "That's more like it, my little budding historian."

"I have another question. Are there any stories about Thomas Jefferson haunting Colonial Williamsburg?"

The guide shook her head. "I've never heard that Mr. Jefferson is a ghost here, although there are many ghost stories throughout Williamsburg. You can go on several tours that will share some of those stories with you. I don't really have any to share with you on this tour."

Once the tour was done, Aunt Leigh suggested, "We can walk around campus a little bit, if you'd like. We'll head back into Colonial Williamsburg later in the evening for one of the shows."

"I do want to see more of the campus, the more up-to-date part of it, but I really want to go shopping. I've been without a mall since we've been in Virginia. Have some sympathy!" cried Tayleigh.

"You can go to a mall anywhere," I declared. "Don't you want to spend more time in the places that are unique to where we are?"

Jason chimed in, "I don't care what we do, although some cannonballs in the hotel pool would be fun."

"Tell you what, Tayleigh, let's take a walk around campus. Near the other end of campus, there's a beautiful forest we can walk through. On the other side of the forest is one of the newer buildings, the College of Education, along with a few clothing stores that I know you'll love," suggested Aunt Leigh. "That leaves swimming out, Jason, but we did spend some time doing that the other day. You never know, though, you may have energy for a late-night dip after the show tonight."

"What show are we going to?" I asked at the same time Tayleigh yelled, "Yippee!"

"Walk and talk, people," commanded Uncle TJ. "Let's head over toward the football field. Then we'll meander back through campus."

"You have your choice of shows tonight," began Aunt Leigh. "We can go learn how to be soldiers in the Revolutionary Army, which means we'll march and get yelled at a few times."

"I don't even care what the other options are, I want that one!" shouted Jason.

Tayleigh added her two cents, "Not my first choice. What other options are there?"

Aunt Leigh continued, "We can participate in a trial that really happened in the early days of America. We'll be part of the jury and get to decide the outcome, and then we'll learn if what we decided actually happened."

"We kind of already did that today," I reminded everyone. "We were in a bit of a mock trial at the Capitol."

"It's more involved than that, Polly," started Uncle TJ. "But, you're right; you have done something along the same vein already. Share another idea, Leigh."

"We can go on a ghost walk and learn about the supposed ghosts that inhabit Colonial Williamsburg, who they were in life, and where we might see a haunting," offered Aunt Leigh.

"Changed my mind!" yelled Jason. "It would be so amazing to catch a ghost on video for our class!"

I concurred with Jason, "It would be fun to film it, but it would be fun to listen to the stories even if we don't see anything. I vote for that one, too." Maybe I would learn something about the ghost that had been following me for the past few days.

Even Tayleigh agreed with us! "I guess it's settled. The ghost walk it is!" stated Uncle TJ as he gestured for us to follow him down the wooded trail toward the College of Education. "Let's walk around campus a bit, and then we can head over to the candy store and get some pizza at Stephano's."

———

I started to follow everyone, but then three gentlemen to my left caught my eye. They were dressed in more formal colonial attire, maybe heading to a meeting or early dinner. I just loved how people in Williamsburg could dress up any time of the day or night and totally fit in. It would have been fun to be in costume there too. If there's a costume store here, maybe we could look at costumes. I know Uncle TJ would love the type of jacket that Thomas Jefferson had on at the conversation yesterday. I looked back at my family for a minute and realized they were moving slowly enough that I could easily catch up, so I hurried over to talk to the costumed men to ask where they bought their costumes.

"Excuse me!" I shouted. "Excuse me, sirs! I'd love to know where you bought your costumes," I shouted as I ran up to them, but they were just ignoring me. I picked up my pace to try to catch up to them. They walked briskly back through the old part of campus and then onto DOG Street, right by the candy store Uncle TJ was talking about earlier. I didn't want to yell at them now with so many people around now, so I decided to tap one of them on the back when I got close enough.

I felt like I'd been running forever, but I just couldn't seem to catch up to them at all. I ran past all of the stores, the church, the courthouse, and some very old shops. I felt like I was running back in time, going from modern to colonial. Finally, the men walked into the King's Arms Tavern. I debated about walking in or not. I was already so far away from where Aunt Leigh and Uncle TJ were, I decided I might as well finish it. I walked into the tavern and didn't see the men anywhere.

"Hi, honey, do you have a reservation?" asked a woman standing at the door inside. "Is your family already inside?"

"No, I'm not here to eat. I followed a couple of men wearing long colonial coats in here. I wanted to ask them where they bought their costumes," I explained.

"Performers aren't allowed to eat in here in costume during the day. That would confuse our patrons. No one has come in here in costume, and I've been standing here for a half hour."

"Seriously? I just saw them walk in here. It was literally a minute before I came in." I looked around but didn't see them anywhere. They really gave me the slip. "I'm sorry to bother you. I must have missed them."

I am going to be in so much trouble. Uncle TJ and Aunt Leigh are probably looking all over for me. I can't even call them since my cell phone doesn't work here. I guess I should head back over to where they last were. Not cool! I'm going to get in trouble and I didn't even get my question answered. If I'd at least found out where the men bought their costumes, maybe everyone would understand.

I started to head back toward the College of William and Mary when I saw the men again. They were heading toward the Capitol. I took off running as fast as I could, yelling at them as I ran, "Excuse me! Hey! Patriotic guys! Please look over here!" I'm sure everyone was staring at me, but I really didn't care. The taller of the men turned his head back to look at me and winked. What? I'm pretty sure that's Phil Parker. Why won't he stop at talk to me, then? He just met me yesterday. I'm sure he remembers me. "Mr. Parker! Please wait a minute!"

The men walked into Charlton's Coffeehouse, just before the Capitol. I'd read somewhere that men during Jefferson's time would meet in coffeehouses for important meetings while also socializing. Maybe these men were part of a play right now, so they were in a hurry to get to where they were going. I decided I could forgive Mr. Parker for that.

I started to open the Coffeehouse door, but a man said I needed to wait for the next tour. "I'm not here for the tour," I said. "I just need to talk to Mr. Parker for a minute."

"Do you mean Mr. Jefferson?" he asked with a smile. I forgot that everyone stayed in character so well there.

"Yes, Mr. Jefferson. I saw him go inside, and I want to ask him a quick question."

"Mr. Jefferson isn't inside. He's probably getting ready for his speech that will take place near the Capitol in an hour or so," explained the doorman.

"Please let me in. I know he's in there. I just saw him go in. I'm not some crazy fan. I actually met him yesterday at Poplar Forest. He knows my aunt and uncle. Please let me go talk to him for a minute," I pleaded.

I must have been pretty convincing because the man nodded and opened the door. "Just be quiet as you walk through the first room. Go to the door in the back of the room on the left and you might find him there, if he is inside."

"Thank you," I whispered as I squeezed inside the crowded room. I quickly walked to the other side of the room and out the door, trying to act like I knew what I was doing. I entered some type of sitting room, and there the men were sitting on several couches, deep in conversation. Finally!

"Mr. Par . . . um . . . Jefferson? Would you mind telling me where you bought your costume? I think my Uncle TJ would love a coat like that, so I want to be able to tell Aunt Leigh where she could buy one and give it to him as a surprise," I quietly asked.

Mr. Parker smiled at me and gestured to the men he was sitting with to wait a minute. Thankfully this detour wasn't made in vain. He was going to tell me!

"I appreciate the finer garments of the day. Several of my favorite waistcoats I purchased while in France and have brought back with me."

"Can you please tell me the name of the place where you bought them so we can look it up on the Internet?" I implored.

I guess Mr. Parker was done talking with me as he turned back to his friends, ignoring me again. I leaned forward to tap him on the arm, but my hand slipped through and landed on the arm of the sofa. I stumbled a bit and then steadied myself on the back of the sofa. I looked back up at Mr. Parker, but all of the men were gone! I quickly looked around and then sat down on the sofa, convinced I was losing my mind.

"What are you doing here, miss? You should be with one of the tour groups. We do not approve of kids gallivanting around on their own," said a woman peering in from a door on the other side of the room. She was wearing the type of dress, full length to the floor, which told me she worked there.

"I don't even know anymore," I conceded.

"Where are your parents?" she asked, more kindly this time.

I shook my head. I didn't even know what to say. I just ditched my family, ran all through Williamsburg, and talked to nobody! Hearing voices made me anxious, but I was getting used to them. Seeing Jefferson's ghost a few times was freaky, but I could still deal with that. This was . . . too much. What was wrong with me?

"Polly," whispered the woman. "Talk to me, honey. Are you okay?"

"Omigosh! You're a ghost, too! How else would you know my name? I'm totally losing my mind!" I screamed. I mean, I screamed loudly. I started thrashing around, pushing the woman's hands off of me.

"Calm down," she ordered. "I am real. There are no ghosts here." I looked up at her, bewildered. "Your name is on your Patriot's Pass to Colonial Williamsburg. Look, it's right there." She pointed to the pass hanging around my neck. I looked down and breathed deeply. She was right.

"I'm so sorry, ma'am. I'm just a little freaked out right now. I lost my family," I sobbed. I was freaked out, but she didn't need to know the real reason.

"Come on, Polly. Let me take you to security, and we'll find your family. I'm sure they're just as worried about you," she said. "My name is Shelley. I'll stay with you. Just calm down."

I was whisked into another room and out the back of the building. She led me over to a house nearby and got on the phone to call security. I didn't really pay attention to what she was saying. I couldn't help thinking about everything that had happened to me on the trip. I was used to daydreaming time away, but this didn't feel like Polly World.

Shelley was tapping my hand and saying, "Polly, your family has been looking for you too. We're going to meet them over at the Tucker House. Come on, let's go. I'm sure they're very worried about you." I let her lead me down the street, really not paying attention to anything.

"Polly Ann Vesper, don't you ever do that to us again!" shouted Aunt Leigh as she ran down the walk in front of the Tucker House. "We were terrified! Thank God you're okay." She hugged me so tightly. That felt good. She was real. I hugged her back, not wanting to let go.

Everyone hugged me, even Jason. I guess they were really worried. "We've been looking all over for you," said Uncle TJ. "Where were you? What were you thinking? Why did you run off?"

Aunt Leigh pulled me to her side. "Enough, TJ. Let's go inside and sit down. We don't need to discuss all of this with an audience." She looked around, and I noticed that a few people had stopped walking and were looking at us. "Go on, kids, go inside. Thank you so much for finding Polly," she said as she turned to Shelley.

"She was pretty upset when she realized she wasn't with you all," Shelley offered. "I'm just glad everyone has been reunited. I better get back to the Coffeehouse." With that, she walked back toward the Capitol.

We walked inside the Tucker House and sat down in a sitting room similar to the one I'd seen inside the Coffeehouse.

I looked at Uncle TJ and then at Aunt Leigh, seeing concern and anger on both of their faces. I couldn't blame them. "I wasn't freaked out because I was alone," I started. "I was freaked out because I realized I was chasing a ghost or vision or something my crazy mind created. I think I'm losing my marbles!" I started crying again, softly this time, not my hysterical sobs of earlier. "Can I tell you something without you just laughing at me?"

"I don't think any of us are in a laughing mood right now," stated Uncle TJ.

I nodded and went ahead with my story. I explained everything to them. I knew Jason wanted to say something a few times, probably to make fun of me, but he thought better of it and kept his mouth shut. I told them about the voice I kept hearing, telling me information about Thomas Jefferson but speaking to me as if he was Jefferson. I told them about seeing Thomas Jefferson. I told them about chasing Jefferson and a few other men through the streets of Colonial Williamsburg. I paused, looking to Uncle TJ and Aunt Leigh to gauge their reactions, hoping they didn't think I was crazy.

Aunt Leigh thought for a minute and then asked, "When did you first hear the voice?" I didn't realize I was holding my breath until I let it out in a whoosh when she spoke. She didn't think I was crazy! Or at least she was humoring me enough to think it through with me.

"I'm pretty sure we were at Monticello. I think we were in the library or bedroom when I first heard Jefferson's voice. I thought for sure it was Uncle TJ, but it wasn't. The voice told me that Jefferson put his feet in ice cold water every morning because he thought it was good for his health."

"Good starting point," said Aunt Leigh. "Now, let's think what you were doing before that. Something that might have triggered you to start hearing this voice. I'm not making fun of you, but are you sure you checked your iPod to make sure Jason or someone didn't fiddle with it so it spontaneously speaks Jefferson quotes out loud?"

"I did check my iPod. I don't think these are quotes anyway. Sometimes the voice is very conversational. Sometimes I feel like he's talking directly to me, and other times I feel like he's thinking out loud and I just get to overhear him. Before we went into Monticello, we were just hanging around the Visitor's Center. Wait, I made a wish at the water! That's got to be it. How come I didn't think of that before? You even warned me to be careful what I wished for because of your history with wishes," I said, turning to Tayleigh, who vigorously nodded.

"I totally believe in the power of wishes," said Tayleigh.

"What did you wish for?" asked Jason.

"I threw a nickel into the fountain, thinking a nickel might be extra lucky because pictures of Jefferson and Monticello are on it, and I wished that I'd know some things on this trip about Jefferson that Uncle TJ doesn't know. He knows everything about Jefferson, and I just wanted to impress him. That has to be it. Somehow my wish came true."

Aunt Leigh said, "I can't even speculate why this wish would come true. I've thrown my share of change in fountains over the years, but none of my wishes have come true. Or, if they have, I didn't realize it was because of my wish. How bizarre if it was the combination of the nickel at Monticello and just the right wish at the right time."

"Thank you for believing in me. Even if I'm still crazy and will end up in an institution because I hear voices and see things, I appreciate you taking some time to think this through with me so I don't feel so crazy right now," I said. I had tears in my eyes. It had been a lot more stressful than I'd realized. I enjoyed knowing facts and impressing Uncle TJ, but it was hard being the only one who could hear the voice.

"We're always here for you, Polly. I wish you'd share all of this a lot sooner so you didn't have to deal with it all by yourself," replied Uncle TJ. "This whole situation could have been avoided if you'd been honest with us. Instead, you've been feeling alone on this trip, we've wasted a lot of time at Williamsburg, and everyone had a scare. We were very worried about you. And honestly, since we've found you, I've been questioning if we should have taken you all on this vacation. I thought you were more responsible than this." I could tell he was so disappointed in me. It was not a feeling I liked.

"I didn't do anything!" whined Jason. "Don't lump us all in the same group. Tay and I were with you the whole time."

Aunt Leigh reached over and took Uncle TJ's hand. She looked each of us directly in the eyes and said, "TJ is just upset about what happened, as am I. Of course we're very fortunate that we could take you on vacation, and we love spending time with you. The thought of anything happening to any of you is just terrifying. We've had a few little crazy episodes this trip, including you hurting your ankle, Jason, and you not wanting to be with us for a while, Tayleigh. It just makes us wonder if it was the right choice to take this trip. We don't want to be responsible for anything bad happening to any of you."

"We're all fine, Aunt Leigh!" urged Tayleigh. "Please don't give up on us, Uncle TJ. It's been a great trip for the most part."

"I think we need to do something quiet for the evening," suggested Aunt Leigh. "Let's skip the ghost tour and head back to the hotel. We can go swimming and relax."

—<><>—

We headed back to the hotel, which was probably the best idea. No one really seemed mad at me anymore, but there was still some tension in the air. I had to figure out how to make things right or it was going to be a long trip home the next day.

"Why don't you get ready for a swim?" suggested Aunt Leigh. "TJ and I are going to take a little walk first to talk about some things."

Uh-oh. This is where they decide how they're going to punish me for running off. I deserve it, I know. I'll take whatever punishment they give me. I just hope they aren't mad at me for long. I wondered if they'd told my parents about any of it.

"Hurry up and change," ordered Tayleigh as she pushed me off the edge of the bed. "We don't want to be waiting on you again."

I finished changing as Uncle TJ and Aunt Leigh walked back into the room. "Before we head to the pool, we really need to call your parents and tell them what happened today. We didn't call them earlier because we didn't want to worry them unnecessarily since there wasn't anything they could do from afar. Now that everyone is safe, we need to explain to them what happened," explained Uncle TJ.

"I'll do it," I said. I needed to own up to what happened. I called Mom and Dad and explained everything to them, including the voices and visions. I told them how badly I felt for disappointing everyone. I kept telling myself not to cry again. Uncle TJ motioned for me to give him the phone when I was done.

"Yes, it's been quite a day," he started. "Leigh and I were just talking, though, and we don't want this trip to end on a sour note. I said something earlier when I was upset. I made the kids feel like I regretted bringing them on this trip, but I don't. I have loved spending time with them. The trip has been fun for the most part, and we'd like to continue that for another day, giving everyone a chance to prove that bringing them was the right choice."

We were all ears. What was he talking about?

Uncle TJ continued, "We just don't feel it's right to be so close to Washington, DC, and not stop by for a quick visit. Obviously we won't be able to see much in one day, but the kids can get a taste for what's in our nation's capitol. We could drive home all night on Sunday so the kids are there for school on Monday, or we could spend another night and be home Monday evening. We haven't done anything about this; in fact, the kids are hearing this for the first time as I'm telling you. I'd have to call my boss to get another day off approved, but I think it'll be okay since I haven't taken any vacation days in a long time. Leigh said she can be flexible on Monday as well . . . okay, just a minute."

Uncle TJ put his phone down and hit the speakerphone button so we all could hear.

"Do any of you have any big assignments due on Monday or tests?" asked Mom. None of us did as far as we knew.

"What about rehearsals for dance, band, choir, or anything?" asked Dad. Tayleigh did have that dance to plan for nationals, but she said it wasn't critical that she be at practice on Monday.

"Don't you guys have a youth group event coming up that you should be planning?" continued Mom.

"We do, Mom, but Amber and I already have most of it planned, and she's been working on a few things while we've been gone. It's all under control, Mom, really," Tayleigh explained.

"Okay, then, it sounds okay to us. TJ, thanks for being willing to drive home Sunday night. I know that's an extra burden on you and Leigh, but I'd really hate to see them miss another day of school. I know they're learning a lot about history during this trip, but I'd prefer they get back to school," Dad shared.

"You all need to be on your best behavior and convince TJ and Leigh they made the right choice in taking you on vacation," Mom commanded.

"We will!" we chorused.

We were lucky. I totally got that. We said our good-byes to Mom and Dad after spending a few minutes telling them about the better points of the day.

"Let's go take that swim now. Move it!" yelled Uncle TJ when we got off the phone. I don't think I've ever seen Jason move so fast!

I walked over to Uncle TJ and gave him a big hug. "Thank you," I said as I looked up at him.

"Don't scare me like that again. Love you," he said as he hugged me back.

Yep, I was lucky.

7

Washington, DC

It wasn't that bad of a drive to Washington, DC. We left really early, so we even beat the rush hour traffic. We were in the downtown area by eight o'clock. On the way to DC, we talked about what each of us would like to do. With only one day in the city, it was so hard to decide. There were monuments and museums and parks and shopping and restaurants and so much to do! We each got to pick one thing we absolutely wanted to do, and we were going to try to fit it all in. Jason wanted to go to the Smithsonian's Air and Space Museum. Tayleigh wanted to go to the top of the Washington Monument. Uncle TJ wanted to go to the Jefferson Memorial and the National Archives—he couldn't pick just one. Aunt Leigh wanted to go to the Library of Congress. I couldn't decide between the White House and the Capitol; but then we found out that you have to make reservations for a White House tour in advance, so my choice ended up being the Capitol. That would be a lot of walking to go to all of those places—about four miles! I just hoped Jason's ankle would hold up. We also found out that most places closed at five, so we'd have to get moving quickly to see everything.

We decided to start at the Jefferson Memorial because it was the farthest in one direction and we could see it at any time because it was outside. We might be there before the gift shop opened, but I doubted we'd have much time for shopping. We parked close to the Memorial, so we had a short walk to start.

The Jefferson Memorial in Washington, DC.

"It's much bigger than I thought it would be, and it reminds me of the ice house at Montpelier," said Jason.

Uncle TJ laughed. "I can totally see that. Uncle Henry would appreciate that comment, too. Just wait until we walk up to the top and you see just how tall President Jefferson was. Of course, it's a life-sized statue."

"Yeah, sure," chuckled Jason. "I'll race you to the top." He took off without waiting for anyone to agree to race. I guess his ankle felt a lot better; maybe the bandage and ice really helped.

"Normally I'd yell at him for running, but there's no one around. If he wants to tire out at our first stop, let him. Just know that I'm not carrying him anywhere!" said Aunt Leigh. "I hope he doesn't fall again."

Jason made it to the top way ahead of any of us. He'd read most of the writings on the wall by the time we got up there too. He even filmed us walking up the last few steps, and then turned around to show the statue of Jefferson. I walked in front of him filming and said, "The mythical giant himself, President Thomas Jefferson. People said he was bigger than life, and here is evidence that he was!" I pointed to the top of Jefferson's head.

"That was perfect, Polly!" he exclaimed. "Our teacher is going to want to send us on other trips to make educational videos everywhere. This may be the start of a career for me. I never thought of being in the movies, but I could totally be a director." We wandered around the statue as Jason continued rambling about how he was going to be famous someday.

"I would hope that people will remember me for my contributions to the tenets of political freedom, religious freedom, and intellectual freedom. I ask that my tombstone be inscribed with 'author of the Declaration of American Independence, of the Statute of Virginia for religious freedom, and Father of the University of Virginia.' While I am proud of my time as president, I believe the documents and institutions I helped develop will have a longer impact on our society."

The voice didn't even bother me this time. I felt so much better after telling everyone about it. "I think Thomas Jefferson would care more about what he did rather than the monuments made about him," I said. The wish, a ghost, Polly World, a brain tumor . . . who knew what this all was, but I just didn't feel so worried about it any more.

Uncle TJ nodded. "I concur. Jefferson was an extremely private man. He didn't seek accolades, and he had very specific requests in how he wanted to be remembered. However, he was such an important part of our history, if we didn't have a huge memorial dedicated to him, many people might forget about his contributions."

Tayleigh guffawed, "No one would forget Jefferson. He wrote the Declaration. That's like USA 101. Everyone knows that."

"You would think that's true, wouldn't you?" posed Aunt Leigh. "You three may be more aware of what's in the Declaration than most kids your age, but I imagine you even know more about it than most adults. I bet if you asked ten people on the street now what the name of the current president is, at least two of them wouldn't tell you the right answer."

"No way!" said Jason. "How can anyone not know who our president is if you live in the USA?"

"Let's do it," I suggested. "Let's film people as we're asking them. It can be part of our video for class. We can test the American public like they do on TV."

"Let's ask a question specifically about Jefferson," continued Jason. "Because our whole trip is about Jefferson, that makes more sense. What could we ask?"

"What number president was Thomas Jefferson?" offered Tayleigh.

Jason and I both smiled. "Perfect," said Jason. "It's an easy enough question, but I bet we get tons of wrong answers."

"Just so we all know, he was the third president, right?" I asked. Aunt Leigh nodded in agreement. "I just wanted to make sure."

We quickly went underneath the Jefferson Memorial for a view of the displays and gift store. When we entered the large room, I heard Jefferson's voice again, but he sounded like he was talking from further away. Every time I heard him before, the voice had been right next to me or even inside my head.

"Do you hear Jefferson's voice in here?" I whispered to Aunt Leigh.

"We all hear it this time," she said with a smile. "Follow me." She led me over to a video that had President Jefferson talking. That voice was so comforting to me now. It sounded like an old friend. I sat down on a marble bench near the video to listen.

"Come on, no time to dawdle," stated Jason as he walked by me, grabbing my arm to pull me with him.

We left the Jefferson Memorial and started walking toward the Washington Monument. Aunt Leigh got online with her phone to get us tickets so we wouldn't have to wait in the long line when we got there. I asked three people along the way our question, a young couple and an older gentleman. The older man got it right, but the young couple wasn't sure if he was the second, third, or fourth president. They knew Washington was the first, so I had to at least give them credit for that. Jason was going to have fun editing that because they were confused bantering back and forth.

"Is it true that the Masons built the Washington Monument as some kind of temple?" asked Tayleigh. "There are so many movies and shows about the Masons now, but I don't know which parts are true and which parts are just Hollywood."

"It's kind of like the secret societies we were talking about at the University of Virginia," added Jason.

Aunt Leigh agreed, "Similar, definitely. We know more about the societies at U.Va., I think. So much about the Masons is still unclear. There's mystery surrounding them, and I honestly don't know what's real anymore. I've read so much about the Masons, the Knights Templar, and the Illuminati that it's all a blur. Suffice it to say that there were many Masons among our founding fathers, but that doesn't mean that everything built around here has some mystical meaning. There are some amazing stones laid inside the Washington Monument that we'll get to see as we ride down the elevator, but that's probably the closest to anything mysterious that we'll be figuring out there."

"Do you think we'll feel it swaying up at the top? I don't like feeling queasy," I said while rubbing my stomach.

Uncle TJ shook his head. "I don't think you have anything to worry about. Now let's get in the line to the elevator." We ran up into the line. It was a beautiful view just looking up while standing next to the Monument with all the flags blowing around. We could stand in one place and see the Lincoln Memorial, the White House, and the Capitol. Pretty cool!

We crammed into the elevator with about ten other people, and Jason nudged me with his iPod in hand. I turned to the girl next to me, who looked to be about my age. "Hi, my name is Polly. I'm from Battle Creek, Michigan. We're filming a video about our vacation for school. Can I ask you a question while my brother films us?" I asked her.

"Um, sure," she said. "I'm Laura, by the way."

"Thanks, Laura! Are you ready, Jase?" I asked, turning to him. He nodded, so we continued. "Laura, can you tell me what number president Thomas Jefferson was?"

The Washington Monument in Washington, DC.

"Doesn't everyone know that? Washington, Adams, Jefferson, Madison, and Monroe. We even learned a song about the order of the presidents," she replied smiling.

"I told you that school-age kids probably know that information better than most adults," commented Aunt Leigh.

"That was great, Laura. You can help make our generation look smart on the video," laughed Jason.

I asked her if she wanted to walk around together when we got to the top. Her parents said it was okay, as long as we didn't go back down the elevator without them. It was nice to meet someone my age. Turned out we had a lot in common too. She was also a dancer, but her favorite type was ballet, and my favorite is hip hop. My favorite thing about the top of the Washington Monument wasn't really the view, it was the pictures of the old views. I could see how DC came to be, and I could compare it to what it looked like now. So many things had changed, but so much was still the same. I took a ton of pictures, including some with Laura and me together. We even exchanged e-mails and cell numbers. Another texting buddy—yeah! She lived in Tennessee, so I doubted I'll see her for a long time. It was still cool to have a friend in another state.

On the ride down in the elevator, the glass cleared up in certain areas so we could see the stones that Aunt Leigh was telling us about. We found a stone for Michigan. It seemed like every state had a stone. Someday it would be fun to walk down the stairs so I could see the stones up close. They were extremely intricate, and we only got to see them for a few seconds because we were going down so quickly.

"It was great to meet you, Laura. I'll friend you on Facebook too! We're heading over to the Air and Space Museum now. Enjoy DC!" I said as I waved to her.

"We're going to the Lincoln Memorial. I guess that's the other way. Bye!" she shouted as she left with her family.

"I'm glad you're so friendly," said Aunt Leigh. "Did I ever tell you about the friends I made in Wisconsin when I was three years old?" We all groaned. There are some stories that adults have to tell repeatedly, no matter how many times we've heard them. They think every time is the first time. The stories change sometimes, but they're consistent for the most part.

Thankfully Uncle TJ intervened, "Leigh, they all know that story. Let's book it to the Smithsonian. We can grab a quick lunch while we're there."

—❧—

I don't think anyone has gone through a museum as quickly as we went through the Air and Space Museum. We didn't get to see any of the shows they offered, but we saw spaceships and planes galore! Some were much smaller than I'd imagined, and some were much bigger. We ate lunch there, including freeze-dried ice cream like the astronauts eat. I used to think being an astronaut would be fun, but I changed my mind after trying their food. Ewwww!

We rushed on to the Capitol next. We were lucky it was such a beautiful day because walking along the Mall wasn't so bad. It wasn't too crowded, either. I liked looking at the different architecture of the buildings. Everything was so huge there. I realized Aunt Leigh was talking, so I started paying attention. ". . . just too bad. I'm sure the Representative Timberg would have given us a personal tour," said Aunt Leigh.

"What can you do when we make a last-minute change like this? He won't even be in his office because it's Sunday. Don't worry about it. The public tour will at least give the kids a taste of what the House and Senate are like," Uncle TJ said. "Who knows, maybe we'll get to go into one of the chambers because the senators and congressmen aren't here working today."

"I want to sit where the president of the Senate sits," stated Jason. "After my long, illustrious career as a filmmaker, I'll probably be a senator or something like that."

People called *me* the dreamer?

The US Capitol in Washington, DC.

After watching a quick video about the Capitol, our official tour started. I didn't know how anyone could work there. I would get lost so quickly. It wasn't just one building. Most of the major buildings in DC are connected by underground tunnels. Just more opportunities for me to get lost, I thought. I'd heard there are tunnels under Disney World too. Maybe all great places have underground tunnels.

"I was the first president to be inaugurated in Washington, DC. It was an honor to have Chief Justice Marshall conduct my inauguration in the Senate chamber."

I wondered if it was called Washington, DC in Jefferson's day. I mean, George was his friend. It would be weird to name a city after a living person, right? I'd have to ask someone about that. We were walking underneath the main part of the Capitol. The tour guide said there used to be some different displays and statues in the room, but they were moved to the new visitor's center. She also said the marking in the middle of the room was called the zero compass stone, and it marked the center of DC. Maybe Jefferson walked across that spot. Was it part of the building then or just dirt? Maybe I'd just keep some of my questions to myself.

The next room we went into was huge! The ceiling was vaulted with paintings on it, there were paintings hung around the room, and there were many statues in the room as well. I could imagine performing a dance in there. It would make for an excellent stage. Very grand. It even had a grand name—the Rotunda.

"Film me by the statue of Jefferson," directed Jason. "I want to tell the class a bit about the Capitol."

"Make sure you mention the zero compass stone that we walked across. Hurry up already. I want to stay with our tour."

In another room, we learned about a special effect that occurs because of the way the room was made. Two people stand at opposite sides of the room and whisper toward the wall, and then each can hear the other clearly. Jason took the iPod and stood at one end while I whispered to the class from the other end. The class might think we dubbed in the sound, but we could explain it to them. There's a rumor that when John Quincy Adams was a representative, he would look like he was falling asleep, when really he was listening to the whispers from the other side of the floor. Sneaky!

"We didn't get a chance to see some of the more private areas of the Capitol, but did you know that they have a full cafeteria, a gym, salon, and other services along the basement corridors?" asked Uncle TJ.

"Wow, it's like they work in a mall, just a really grand one!" exclaimed Tayleigh. "I could totally be in Congress."

"I wouldn't go that far, but the services are located here so they don't have to leave the area. It encourages our representatives to spend more time working for us," explained Aunt Leigh. "I bet you could get everything you need within these walls for weeks at a time. I know Representative Timberg even sleeps in his office just to save money."

"They probably have huge, fancy offices with bedrooms and everything," offered Jason.

"Not all of them," answered Uncle TJ. "The more senior, more experienced congressmen and congresswomen have the fancy offices, but the newer people have fairly small offices. I doubt anyone has an actual bedroom."

"Do we still have time for the Library of Congress?" asked Tayleigh. "It's almost three."

"Let's scoot on over there and see. I sure hope so. It's my absolute favorite place in all of DC. Just wait until you see the art and sculptures. The books themselves are so impressive, but the building is just amazing," said Aunt Leigh.

"It'll be quicker through the tunnels; then they can see the exterior of the building when we're done with the tour," suggested Uncle TJ. "I'm still hoping we can get into the National Archives before they close at five."

The tunnels? I had to tell myself that I wasn't claustrophobic—at least I didn't think I was. I was glad we'd only be in the tunnels for a short while. I'd get lost if I had to work there. How can you have any sense of direction when you're underground in tunnels that all look the same? Okay, sure, there were signs. I don't know, those tunnels just gave me the creeps. There wasn't a lot on the walls, I couldn't see any landmarks, and it looked like the tunnel went on forever. Breathe, Polly, breathe. It'll be okay. Great, now I'm imagining something scary jumping out at me around a corner. I'm going to give myself nightmares. My imagination can turn off at any time now. I need to focus on Jason. He's filming us walking. I'm not sure we'll use any of that for the video for class, especially if I look as panicked as I feel.

I jumped when Aunt Leigh put her arm around me. "How are you doing? You look a little jumpy. Are you hearing the voice right now?" she whispered.

"I'm just freaking out about these tunnels. I definitely don't like them," I explained. "I haven't heard the voice down here, but I have heard it a few times today. I don't mind as much now that I've told you about it."

"I'm sure there will be a logical explanation we'll figure out at some point, but I say we just enjoy the additional knowledge you're bringing to the trip until then." I just smiled at her. "Now just stay with us."

"Come on, everyone, here's our door," announced Uncle TJ. We walked through a door, out of the tunnels, and into the basement of the Library of Congress.

"Welcome to the Thomas Jefferson Building. Go ahead and join the tour at the top of the stairs," the docent said. "You've missed the introduction, but it's the last tour of the day, so it's your only opportunity."

"We'll take it. Thank you," said Uncle TJ. "Come on, everyone, and be quiet as we join the group. You can take pictures, by the way."

"I thought we were going to the Library of Congress, not another Jefferson building," I said. I didn't care where we were, just as long as we were out of that tunnel!

"The main building for the Library of Congress is called the Thomas Jefferson Building. We'll learn more about that on the tour," whispered Aunt Leigh.

"I was happy to help rebuild the library in our Capitol. I believe our congressmen need to have access to books so they can study every topic. Besides, I was already quite far in debt, and the $23,950 helped pay off part of it."

Amazing doesn't even describe it. Fantastic. Unbelievably gorgeous. No words do it justice. The building itself is a museum of art. Aunt Leigh has always said she could spend days in there just staring at the walls and ceilings, and now I understood why. Our tour barely even focused on the books. We got to look in the main library room briefly, but you needed to have special library cards to actually go in there. We did get to see some of the original books that Jefferson sold to start the Library of Congress, but they were behind bulletproof glass. Jefferson had books in many languages and on so many different topics. Jason wanted to film the old books, but we weren't allowed to take any pictures. We did take lots of pictures of angels and quotes and cherubs. I planned to use some of my money to buy a book about the building, if the gift shop was still open when we were done.

**The ceiling in the entry way at the Library of Congress
in Washington, DC.**

"This place is called the Library of Congress. Do the congressmen really come here to check out books?" Tayleigh asked our guide.

"That doesn't happen too often anymore, at least not in person," he answered. "The books stored in this building are only part of the entire collection. We have several other warehouses full of books. The congressmen fill out book requests, and then the books are retrieved and delivered to their offices. It makes the whole process a lot smoother. Otherwise, we'd have people wandering around here, never finding what they were looking for."

Wow, more books. It made sense. If every book was supposed to be there, it sure would take up so much space to keep a copy of all books. I was sure it wasn't every book though, because that would fill up the whole city! Most stuff is on the Internet anyway.

"I didn't really like the Capitol because it seemed like a maze inside. This building makes more sense to me because it's all centered around this big open space. I think I could work here," I said to Tayleigh.

"Remember all the books? We didn't even go in those rooms. I'm sure there are tons of other rooms that may make it all seem like a maze where the books are stored," suggested Tayleigh.

"I hadn't thought of that. You're probably right. Well, I could give tours out there, or I could just sit on the steps all day and stare at the walls," I dreamed.

"Now you're sounding like Aunt Leigh," laughed Jason. "We can leave the two of you here, but I'd rather go find some food."

"We're grabbing a quick taxi, so everyone move it," shouted Uncle TJ as he was running toward the street. "The National Archives are still open for a half hour, so I want to try to get you guys in there. It's only a few blocks away, but we'll save time with a taxi."

Luckily, a taxi stopped quickly, so we were over to the National Archives in no time. There was a long line coming out of the door, so we weren't sure if we could even still go in. Aunt Leigh went over to talk to a security guard. When she came back, she explained, "They allow everyone who's in line by five o'clock to go inside. However, we'll only have a few minutes to look at the documents. I wish we had more time, but we tried to fit so much into one day."

"At least the kids will be able to say they saw the original Declaration of Independence, the Constitution, the Bill of Rights, and even the Louisiana Purchase. There are many more documents there, but you'll hopefully get a chance to look at a few of the big ones," Uncle TJ said in a rush.

"Saying it that fast doesn't make the line move any faster," laughed Aunt Leigh. "Take a deep breath. We'll get in. We may only see one document, but we'll see something."

"They're not the real documents, right? Those papers are so old, they'd have to be all fallen apart by now," Tayleigh stated.

"They're real. Some are in better shape than others though. When you look at the Declaration of Independence, notice how faded all the signatures are. You can barely see where Thomas Jefferson signed it. Other documents, like the Constitution, are in much better shape. Maybe we learned how to take care of important documents in a better way during those few years," Uncle TJ explained. We'd all seen a fairly accurate copy of the Declaration hanging in Uncle TJ and Aunt Leigh's living room, so it didn't matter that much to me to see some faded piece of paper.

The line moved quickly, and soon enough we were inside. It was very dark in there. Uncle TJ said light could damage the old documents. It made it feel very eerie. "I wish I could film in here," bemoaned Jason. "This place is giving me a creepy vibe, but it makes it seem like what we're about to see is extra special." He nailed it. I didn't like the low light, but Jason was right—it did make everything feel more exciting.

"I wrote diligently for several days. I wanted to ensure that our voice was heard by the world in declaring our independence. Franklin and Adams were most helpful in making revisions to the document. However, I was saddened by the many items that were removed or changed by the other members of the Continental Congress, but our primary purpose remained true."

"I didn't know Jefferson had help writing the Declaration," I said to Uncle TJ.

"There were five men appointed to a committee to write the document. Jefferson did the majority of the writing, and then Benjamin Franklin and John Adams helped with some editing. Robert Livingston and Roger Sherman were also members of that committee, but they're often forgotten by the general public."

"I won't forget them," I murmured. "They must have all been great men." We finally got a chance to walk up to the documents, which were all under glass. It was difficult to see anything because of the low light and the faded writing, but it was impressive being that close to something that had been around for hundreds of years.

We walked out of the Archives a little after five o'clock. "I'm still hungry," said Jason.

"We know," laughed Aunt Leigh. "I hope you guys feel like you got a little taste of things in DC, and you'll come back someday to do more. I almost feel like we cheated you by trying to rush so many things into one day."

"I loved it all!" I squealed. "I'm glad we saw so much, but I'm also glad we filmed so much it so we can go back and see some things more clearly."

Aunt Leigh nodded. "I think you'll have to make two videos—one for family memories and one for class. I'm quite positive that some of the things that have been filmed are not necessarily class material." I chuckled along with her.

"You still need a few more people for your presidential question, so how about we take a ride on the Metro?" suggested Uncle TJ.

"Sounds great! Where will we go?" asked Jason.

"I think you've probably had enough history for today, and most of the other places we'd like to take you to are closed now. How about we ride the Metro over to the mall and find some place to have dinner?" suggested Uncle TJ. I grinned as I saw the expressions of satisfaction on Tayleigh and Jason's faces. Tayleigh and a mall . . . Jason and food.

A few Metro stops later and we had all the information we needed from the people on the street. We asked twelve people about President Jefferson, and only five of them knew for sure that he was the third president. Crazy.

8

Going Home

I texted Allie that we were on the road home, only ten hours away. She texted right back and said she couldn't wait to hear about the trip. I hoped she would like what I bought for her. It wasn't much, but it was a little Jefferson memento of our trip. I got us matching TJ necklaces. Uncle TJ said it was because I loved him so much, which I do, but it was really as a reminder of the trip and learning all about Thomas Jefferson—the original TJ. Uncle TJ wanted me to believe that Jefferson was named after him. Not sure what kind of time travel had to happen for that to be true. He's just so silly!

"Before everyone falls asleep, including me—" started Uncle TJ.

Aunt Leigh interrupted, "Wait a minute! If you're seriously tired already, I'll start driving."

"Just kidding, relax. I'll drive for a while. Now, what was your favorite thing about this trip?" asked Uncle TJ.

"Everything isn't a good enough answer, is it?" asked Tayleigh.

"You know you can't," answered Aunt Leigh. "Remember, we need details."

"I know my favorite part, although I agree with Tay that everything was great. My favorite thing, though, was at the University of Virginia when we saw the markings of the secret societies and learned about them. I want to know more about them. I also have some ideas for some videos I might make and put up on YouTube," explained Jason.

"I'll have to get Bryant to help me with that because I've never put anything on YouTube before."

"Excellent, Jason. I'd love to help you with the videos too," offered Uncle TJ. "Secret societies are fun, and you got to experience some of it firsthand."

"I wanted to like Colonial Williamsburg, but it was a little cold and I just wasn't too into things that day. Plus, Polly pretty much ruined the afternoon. I think my favorite part of Williamsburg was the College of William & Mary. I liked how they kept the old but still had new things around so students could still be on the cutting edge," said Tayleigh.

Aunt Leigh looked thoughtful. "Hmmm . . . maybe we should have just done a college tour. So far the kids like the colleges the best."

"But they're colleges that go along with the theme of the trip, Aunt Leigh. Other colleges wouldn't have worked for this trip," said Jason.

"Good point," she agreed. "What about you, Polly?"

"I don't think I can pick just one. I've loved the whole trip. I know, I know . . . I can't just say that. I'm going to have to pick two though. I honestly can't choose between them. I thought the Dome Room at Monticello was simply magical. I could almost see Jefferson's granddaughters playing in there. I also loved the conversation at Poplar Forest between Jefferson and Madison. I thought it would be boring, but I felt like I traveled back in time to listen to those great men. They were so funny!"

"Good choices, and well said," commented Uncle TJ.

"What was your favorite thing, Uncle?" I asked. I wanted to make sure he and Aunt Leigh got to share too.

"I love almost everything about Jefferson, and we've been to most of the places on this trip before. I'd have to say that my favorite thing about this trip was seeing everything through your eyes. Tayleigh has come to Virginia with us before, but it was a much shorter trip. Seeing the three of you get excited about history and make connections to the world today—that was just priceless. I hope you've developed a love of history that will last your whole life. As Polly knows, I've always loved history, but your aunt hasn't. She didn't start loving history until she was an adult," Uncle TJ told us.

"It's true." Aunt Leigh nodded.

"I hope you don't have to wait that long to really love it. Maybe as you learn more about events that happened in history, you can think back to this trip and those events will seem more real to you. You'll understand that they actually did happen, they're not just stories we read," continued Uncle TJ. "I love that you loved this trip."

"Can I just agree with your favorite thing? It was so well stated," said Aunt Leigh.

"That's not fair," whined Jason. "You have to come up with your own idea . . . with details."

"I loved it all too, and I loved going on this trip with all of you. I think something that made this trip special—and gave us a little more insight than we'd normally have—was a wish made at Monticello. So, I'll say that my favorite part of this trip was all the Jefferson information that Polly was able to share with us throughout the trip," contributed Aunt Leigh.

I'm sure I was turning red. I was a little embarrassed that she brought it up, but then I was also a little pleased that she thought it made the trip better. "I'm just glad you believed me," I whispered.

"I still think you're crazy, but I guess I believe you," taunted Jason. I turned around and punched him in the leg.

"It'll be interesting to find out if you still hear those voices when we get home," said Uncle TJ. "I know you wished to find out details about Jefferson while we were on the trip, so will the voice stop when the trip is over?"

"I wish to spend my remaining days at Monticello with family and friends. There is no greater place to be than at home."

"Who knows. I think Jefferson would have been happy that we're heading home. With a home like Monticello, I think he liked to be home a lot," I replied. I was used to the voice and ghosts now . . . maybe I didn't want them to end.

———◦◦◦———

I was so glad Uncle TJ brought his laptop so we could edit the video on the ride home, but I knew we were all going to have to go to sleep soon so we'd be awake enough for school the next day. We were able to download everything we shot each night, so it was all on the hard drive. Too bad there weren't two keyboards on it so we could work faster.

"My hair is blowing across my face," whined Tayleigh. "Don't use that part." She was referring to her introduction of our trip at the base of Monticello.

"I think you did an excellent job with that, Tayleigh. Don't be so critical of yourself. You can't control the wind," said Aunt Leigh.

Jason stated with authority, "It's staying. This is the director's cut, and I'm the director."

"We're the directors," I corrected.

"Okay. Okay. I want to leave that part in though. It's hard to figure out what to cut out because so much of it was good. I want to take the class on a field trip with us, and if we cut too much out, they'll miss out on part of the trip," explained Jason.

"I have a suggestion," offered Uncle TJ. "You can do a short video, maybe five minutes or so, highlighting parts of the trip. It'll kind of be like a movie trailer where you just get people interested in history and what you learned. You'll definitely need to include some of the questions you asked people on the street. Then, you can also do the full video the way you want it. If the teacher or class decides they want to see the whole video, you'll have it ready. We'll have a fantastic video to watch and remind us of everything we did."

"I like that . . . a movie trailer. We don't have to include all the narration, and we can show some video of places while we're narrating. It can be really fast-paced so we cram a lot into a short time," said Jason.

I continued, "I think the long version of the video probably wouldn't be longer than a half hour anyway, so it's possible that Mrs. Truckey would let us play the whole video in class."

"We'll definitely have a red-carpet event to invite family and friends over to watch it!" announced Aunt Leigh.

"Let's work on the movie trailer version so we can have that done to share in history class tomorrow. Then, if Mrs. Truckey and the class like it, we can bring the full movie in another day. That's just in case we don't finish it on the way home," Jason suggested.

"We have more than nine hours to go. Let's get busy!" I said.

"No, you have two more hours to go. All electronics are getting turned off at ten. You need to get some sleep," said Uncle TJ.

Epilogue

The last time I heard Mr. Jefferson's voice was in the car on the way home. I mean, I heard the voice when Jason played with his talking doll, which he did quite often. I think he did that just to make me think I was going crazy. I'd come to terms with it. I told Allie all about it the next day at school, and she was jealous that she hadn't heard his voice too.

I did find out that Jason had some podcasts on his iPod that had Mr. Parker giving some lectures at Colonial Williamsburg. Maybe it was Jason all along. Maybe Uncle TJ was in on it too. That's totally something they'd do together. Although, I find it hard to believe they never took credit for it. It was a marvelous prank if they did it.

I guess I could have imagined the visions of Thomas Jefferson. I know I "visit" Polly World often, but I usually know I'm daydreaming. Those visions just seemed so real. Maybe it was his ghost. It's a possibility, right? Just because Jefferson isn't part of any ghost tour anywhere we went doesn't mean his ghost isn't out there. Maybe he was just waiting for the right person to talk to—and that was me!

I like to think it was the wish. Maybe the combination of a Jefferson nickel and a fountain at Monticello . . . maybe that did it. Whatever it was, it was fantastically wonderful. I can look back and say that with authority. Having Thomas Jefferson along with us on our trip made our journey much more real to me. I even added a little bit to the end of our family video, highlighting some of the things that Mr. Jefferson told me. I don't want to ever forget them or this trip!